TALES C
TOKOLOSHE

by Pieter Scholtz
illustrated by Cherie Treweek

To: Jackson
With all my love,
Mommy 7/07/06

TALES OF THE
TOKOLOSHE

Published by Struik Publishers (a division of New Holland Publishing (South Africa) (Pty) Ltd)

New Holland Publishing is a member of Johnnic Communications Ltd

Cornelis Struik House, 80 McKenzie Street, Cape Town 8001

86 Edgware Road, London, W2 2EA, United Kingdom

14 Aquatic Drive, Frenchs Forest, NSW 2086, Australia

218 Lake Road, Northcote, Auckland, New Zealand

www.struik.co.za

PUBLISHING MANAGER: Linda de Villiers

MANAGING EDITOR: Cecilia Barfield

EDITOR: Brian Brown

DESIGNER: Beverley Dodd

ILLUSTRATOR: Cherie Treweek

REPRODUCTION: Hirt & Carter Cape (Pty) Ltd

PRINTING AND BINDING: Paarl Print, Oosterland Street, Paarl, South Africa

ISBN 1 86872 970 2

10 9 8 7 6 5 4 3 2 1

www.imagesofafrica.co.za

IMAGES OF AFRICA
PHOTO LIBRARY

Log onto our photographic website **www.imagesofafrica.co.za** for an African experience

CONTENTS

INTRODUCTION

Long, long ago, longer ago than people can remember, the vast continent of Africa was inhabited by tiny creatures called Tokoloshes. Every stream, waterfall and pool had its Tokoloshe, for they were water sprites and couldn't bear to venture very far from the tinkle and ripple of the water.

They took a particular liking to the rivers in the south, in a land called Zululand where rivers had such names as Thukela, Mhlatuze, Mfolozi, Mkhuze and Phongolo, and they gambolled and frolicked in the sparkling streams.

They loved to invent words to describe what they did and the first word they invented was 'fun'. Then they immediately set about giving a meaning to the word and had lots of fun.

The next word they invented was 'mischief' and this was even better because it made them feel naughty (a word they hadn't quite invented yet).

As the Tokoloshes became more inventive the human beings, whom they called 'big ones', became more and more possessive. They wanted to possess the land, built towns, cities and factories, and the Tokoloshes were driven further and further into the far reaches of their streams and rivers.

Some fled the land and found refuge in other countries, where they crept into the minds of poets and writers who then wrote about Tokoloshes, but called them names like 'Puck' and 'Hobbit'. Others found refuge in the company of kindred spirits called leprechauns and gnomes.

Those who remained decided it would be safer to find themselves a human shape, for at that stage they were still gleamings of energy, but they found most human shapes quite boring. Then one day they saw a troupe of monkeys and they immediately knew they had found their corporal form.

And that is how Tokoloshes came to be small, hairy creatures, while retaining the power to change themselves into gleamings of energy and become invisible to human eyes when they chose.

In the southern reaches of Africa, as we have mentioned, is a land that used to be called Zululand but is now called KwaZulu-Natal – a land of rolling hills and fields of green sugar cane where Zulu folk tales (*Izinganekwane*) are told to young children, usually by their grandmother (*Gogo*). The words 'storytelling' and 'folk tales' are important because it is necessary to remember that tales like the ones you will read were told by a Storyteller to a group of young people and adults around the fire.

In Africa, music, poetry and storytelling are a way of life. There are thousands of tales: scary ones and funny ones, tales about animals who can talk (*Ezezilwane*) and tales about clever people who trick greedy ones and teach them a lesson (*Ezeqili*). *Tales of the Tokoloshe* are just such stories and it will become evident when you read them that the little creature known as the Tokoloshe is a mischievous, fun-loving imp, a sprite who causes chaos and consternation through impudence and precocity.

Tokoloshe in these tales enjoys tricks and mischief more than anything in the world and he has two chief ways of making mischief. The first involves a magic pebble he keeps in a small, leather bag around his neck. When he rubs this pebble and chants a weird spell, the most incredible happening occurs: first a sound like the hum of electric cables is heard, then the muscular, hairy form of the Tokoloshe slowly begins to dissolve into a misty, ethereal shape and suddenly the ghostly figure disappears in a shower of sparkling, luminous fire-flies. In this invisible form he is free to range the far reaches of his stream without fear of being detected and, of course, free to perpetrate any form of mischief he pleases.

The second magical trick that enables the Tokoloshe to initiate any manner of mischief is his ability to assume any shape or form he pleases. In his invisible state he is able to enter and become any animal or creature from the tiniest gnat to the most raucous bullfrog or ferocious bull and, when he decides to inhabit that creature, he is able to dictate its behaviour.

For the rest, the tales explore the rich fabric of rural customs and beliefs and follow the Tokoloshe as he sows his seeds of fun and individuality throughout the land.

SOME SUGGESTIONS

Why not read these stories with three or more friends? One can be the Storyteller while the others can read the roles of all the characters who appear in the stories. In this way, through participation (playing a part), you will make the story come alive. You can also read them to your friends or parents and so have an audience.

At the end of the book you will find a Glossary. The word 'glossary' simply means a dictionary of special words. In these stories the special words are mainly the ones that are not English but Zulu, the language spoken by most of the people who appear in the stories. When you come across a word that is not English, look in the Glossary to see what it means.

Finally, you will find some long and difficult words used in these stories. If you don't know what they mean, use a dictionary or ask your parents and then, when you have a chance, see if you can use them in your own conversation.

Pieter Scholtz

ACKNOWLEDGEMENT

In their book *The Abundant Herds, a celebration of the cattle of the Zulu people*, published by Fernwood Press, one of the Nguni cattle identified by the authors, Marguerite Poland and David Hammond-Tooke, is described as *Inkomazi ezikhala zemithi* (the cow which is the gaps between the branches of the trees, silhouetted against the sky).

THE ENCHANTED COW

Tokoloshe wiggled his toes and the moon danced between them like a ping-pong ball. He was lying on his back with his hands behind his head, squinting at his long, knobbly toes, above which the white incandescent ball of the moon was suspended.

He laughed a gurgling laugh – not unlike a monkey's chatter – and spread his big toe sideways to form a 'V' shape, and the ping-pong moon fell neatly into the cleft. Unlike humans, but much like monkeys, Tokoloshes are able to spread their toes like fingers.

Tokoloshe breathed a deep sigh of contentment, closed his eyes, and the moon disappeared in a blink.

He thought back to the events of the day and a satisfied grin creased his face. His first prank had been to turn himself into a river crab and nip the toes of the foolish maidens who had come to bathe in the stream during the heat of noon. Their shrieks and splashing mingled with his chattering laughter, which bubbled to the surface of the pool where they swam.

After terrorising the maidens for some time, Tokoloshe became bored with the game and decided to join the young boys further up the stream, where they were swinging out across the stream on a long vine or monkey-rope and dropping with a mighty splash when the rope reached the height of its arc.

Although Tokoloshe had a muscular, hairy body, he had the face of a mischievous schoolboy with sharp, sparkling eyes and small, pointed ears and, if truth be told, he had much in common with the young boys of the village who accepted him without question.

One of the reasons he felt at one with them was that they were nearer his size and they seemed to enjoy the same games and tricks he did. He did not trust the big ones and when he happened to bump into one of them unexpectedly, he would quickly rub his magic pebble and disappear.

As he lay on the large, flat stone, still warm from the heat of the day, with the stream lapping his head and his shoulders, he relived the pranks of the day and gurgled with delight. He thought life was wonderful!

The breeze freshened and above the faint cry of the fish eagle in the distance, Tokoloshe heard another sound, for Tokoloshe ears are sharp and pointed and can pick up sounds from kilometres away. This was the sound of an argument; it was just a snatch borne by the breeze, but Tokoloshe sat up immediately.

What Tokoloshe heard was an argument between two big ones, a man and a woman, and he heard the woman say: 'What happened last time? You got caught, didn't you?'

And the man responded: 'You always harp on the past, hey? How was I to know they had burglar alarms? This time it's foolproof!'

The breeze had almost died down and all Tokoloshe heard was her faint reply: 'Ya, I've heard that before.'

Tokoloshe's eyes sparkled with anticipation as he sensed there was some mischief afoot and he decided at once to investigate. Just then, he caught sight of some dandelion puffballs that were being wafted by the breeze and immediately decided to catch a lift. He quickly rubbed his magic pebble and in an instant was invisible. Then he made his invisible form as tiny as a gnat and clung to one of the floating puffballs.

'Wheee! This is fun,' he chortled as the puffball swirled and rose in the breeze; it dipped and tumbled on the stream, rolling and bouncing lightly. Then a strong gust of wind scattered the puffball into a myriad, tiny umbrellas, and Tokoloshe clung to one of them and was borne high into the air.

Suddenly, Tokoloshe realized he was being blown in the wrong direction; the breeze that had borne the snatch of argument to his ears was now gusting him further away from the source.

Irritated with himself for being so stupid, Tokoloshe let go of his little umbrella and dropped soundlessly near a pigeon that was strutting about, pouting and puffing out its chest.

THE ENCHANTED COW

The pigeon squawked indignantly when Tokoloshe jumped onto its back; it couldn't see him, but it felt something. Then its neck stretched, its eyes opened wide and its feathers flared as Tokoloshe squeezed inside the form of the pigeon.

It took to the sky like a hawk going after its prey, and then dived down and skimmed along at breakneck speed, just above the surface of the stream.

Inside the pigeon, Tokoloshe could hear the voices more clearly as they approached the source and as they rounded a corner of the meandering stream he saw, through the pigeon's eyes, a wisp of smoke curling upwards from a clearing at the edge of the stream and two figures crouching before a small fire.

Tokoloshe guided the pigeon to a large wild-fig tree, whose branches spread over the clearing, and settled on a branch directly above the fire. Then he popped out of the pigeon, which flapped its wings and squawked noisily before flying off on its bewildered way.

The two figures crouching over the fire broke off their conversation and glanced up at the squawking pigeon, but of course they didn't see the invisible Tokoloshe who now straddled the branch with his little, hairy legs dangling above them.

'Hey, the food's burning,' yelled the woman, pointing at a freshly plucked chicken sizzling on the fire. They had stolen quietly into the yard of a nearby farmer who kept free-range chickens. One had ranged too freely and was now cooking over their fire.

'Don't get excited,' retorted the man as he turned the chicken, 'it's almost right, just a few more minutes.'

The woman put a half-full bottle to her mouth and took a long draught. 'OK, tell me once more about your wonderful plan,' she said.

The man snatched the bottle from her. 'You' had enough,' he snapped.

'Ag, don't be so mean,' she whined, 'tell me again.'

He took a short swig from the bottle and cleared his throat. 'I told you,' he said, 'you never listen! When everybody's asleep we steal into the field where the cattle are grazing. We already know the one we'll take, the grey cow with white patches.'

The woman interrupted, 'An' with black markings on its head.'

'That's right,' retorted the man, 'you do listen sometimes. Then we lead it off quietly and slaughter it in the bush.'

The woman cackled: 'We can sell the meat an' we'll be flush again.'

The man stood up and took the roasted chicken off the coals. 'It's ready,' he said, breaking off a leg and handing it to her. For the next ten minutes they devoured the chicken, smacking their lips and licking their fingers as the hot fat trickled down their chins.

Tokoloshe sat on the branch thinking; he had listened with great interest to their plan and had devised a clever strategy to trick them. He knew the beast they had described, for it was a very distinctive type of indigenous cow known as *Inkomazi ezikhala zemithi*, which meant in Zulu: 'The cow which is the gaps between the branches of the trees, silhouetted against the sky'.

Tokoloshe was beginning to enjoy the prospect of tricking these two scoundrels and he leaped from the branch and landed soundlessly on the mossy bank of the stream.

He diminished his invisible self to a minute size again and mounted a dragonfly that was hovering nearby and, spurring it on one side and then the other to direct it, he rode it like a horse, skimming over the surface of the stream.

When they reached the lush, green field where the cattle were grazing, Tokoloshe leaped off, leaving the angry dragonfly to buzz around in circles, while he sat on the barbed wire fence that enclosed the field and considered what to do.

There were five or six beasts munching mindlessly away at the long kikuyu grass and Tokoloshe immediately saw the cow they had described. The day was beginning to fade and she had settled herself near the stream and was drowsing in the twilight.

Tokoloshe squatted next to her and studied her; the white underbelly and the cloud-grey flanks were in stark contrast to the black markings at the chest and Tokoloshe nodded in agreement; it certainly did look like patches of sky seen through the branches of a tree.

He glanced at the sky, which was rapidly darkening; it was time to act before the *skelms* arrived. He crept close to the ruminating cow, leaped high and his invisible form landed directly on the cow and disappeared inside her.

She immediately stopped chewing and, with wide eyes and flaring nostrils, reared up like a spirited horse and pawed the earth. Gradually Tokoloshe calmed her down until she stood passively awaiting his control.

The minutes stretched into hours, stars perforated the dark sky and little, fat night owls screeched as they swooped on unsuspecting midges and flying insects.

Then a twig snapped and leaves rustled as the two thieves crept through the bushes and reached the field.

'Ag shame, she looks so peaceful,' whispered the woman.

'Don't be soft,' hissed the man, 'think of the bucks!'

She shook her head, 'Ya, but all the same...'

'All the same, nothing.' He drew out a rusty *panga*. 'Just get the sacks ready for the meat.'

The woman took a bunch of knotted sacks from around her waist and laboriously started untying them while the man crept stealthily closer to the cow with his panga raised to strike.

At that moment, without warning, there was an explosion of Tokoloshe mischief!

The cow suddenly lowered her head like a maddened bull and charged the unsuspecting executioner, tossing him high in the air. He landed, screaming, in some thorn bushes, where he lay dazed and bleeding.

The woman turned just in time to receive a mighty and painful kick in the rear as the cow lashed out with its hind legs, sending her hurtling into the stream with a splash and a scream.

The man slowly crawled out from among the thorn bushes, bruised and bleeding. 'It's gone berserk,' he gasped, 'it's possessed!'

Still inside the cow, Tokoloshe grinned. Little did they know how true that last remark was, he thought.

The woman crawled onto the muddy bank, wet and bedraggled. 'A mad cow,' she spluttered. 'I don't believe it! You had to go and choose a mad cow!'

Tokoloshe took his cue from her and snorted and rolled his head and pawed the ground. At this display of madness, the two battered and bedraggled thieves took to their heels, stumbling, falling and berating each other.

'It's all your fault.' The woman's voice was shrill and accusing.

'My fault? It's always my fault,' he whined.

'You chose a mad cow,' she yelled.

'I tell you it was possessed,' he responded.

Their voices faded as they disappeared further into the tangled mangroves bordering the stream.

Tokoloshe detached himself from the cow like a spectre rising from its corporal form and, rubbing his magic pebble, materialized into his Tokoloshe self.

The cow ambled off, bewildered and confused; something had happened that she couldn't altogether grasp.

Tokoloshe bounded and splashed his way upstream, chuckling with delight at his escapade. What a tale he had to tell the other Tokoloshes!

SOMETHING FISHY

His right ear stuck straight up like a crisp *samoosa,* while his left ear drooped like a limp lettuce leaf. Moreover, he had a black patch over his left eye, while his right eye was bright and clear, giving the impression that half his face was asleep, while the other half was wide awake.

He was a mongrel of very mixed breed and when Jabulani first saw him his ribs were protruding, his eyes were sunken in hollow sockets and his stumpy tail was trying desperately hard to wag.

Jabulani knelt down and stretched out his hand and the mongrel slunk hesitantly towards him, like one hoping for a pat, but expecting a blow. Gently, and with infinite patience, Jabulani stroked his head, feeling the bones behind his ears, until the mongrel stopped shivering and Jabulani could sense him relaxing.

Boy and dog stayed quietly together for some minutes, the one gently stroking and the other gratefully responding. At last Jabulani stood up. 'Sorry,' he whispered, 'I have to go now.'

The boy spoke in Zulu, but the language was irrelevant because the dog understood and looked at him with large, pleading eyes. Jabulani shook his head. 'Sorry,' he said, 'you can't come with me, my father would chase you away,' and he turned and walked briskly away. When he reached the brow of the hill he looked back, but the mongrel was nowhere to be seen.

Jabulani walked on with sadness in his heart. He was a kind-hearted boy and hated seeing any creature suffering. He couldn't understand how the other boys enjoyed aiming at birds with their slings and he never joined them on their 'hunts'.

When he reached the stream that wound its way through the valley near his home he paused, sensing that he was being followed. He turned suddenly but could see nothing behind him; he walked over the narrow footbridge that spanned the stream, then ducked behind some thick bushes and waited.

After a few minutes, he saw the mongrel cautiously approaching the bridge; it stopped to appraise the situation, then started crossing. Jabulani stepped out from behind the bushes. 'Go away,' he said, 'stop following me. I told you, you can't come with me.'

The mongrel stopped but didn't run away; he just stood, pleading with his large eyes. 'Voetsek,' said Jabulani roughly. It was a word he didn't like, but he felt he had to get rid of the dog quickly. 'Go home! Voetsek!'

At the word 'Voetsek,' the dog came bounding up to him, wagging its tail furiously. Jabulani backed away. 'Voetsek,' he said, 'go away!' At the repetition of 'Voetsek' the mongrel jumped up against him and started licking his hands.

Suddenly Jabulani understood. 'I don't believe it,' he exclaimed, 'your name is Voetsek!' The dog made a mighty leap at Jabulani, bowling him over and, as he lay spread-eagled on the grass, it started licking his face lovingly. He had made a friend for life.

Eighteen months passed and Voetsek became a permanent addition to the family. At first Jabulani's father was adamant. 'No way,' he said, 'we can't afford him,' but Voetsek soon disarmed him with his large, appealing eyes and his father relented.

Jabulani and Voetsek became inseparable and Voetsek quickly lost his gaunt and skeletal appearance under Jabulani's loving care.

Jabulani had no brothers or sisters and so the dog became a companion and his close friend, and each day when Jabulani walked to school, which was three or four kilometres beyond the stream, Voetsek would lie patiently all day at the small gate to their home, waiting for Jabulani to return.

It was a Saturday when our story starts and there was no school. Jabulani wanted desperately to play for the school football team but had not been picked and had the whole day free.

Apart from football he had another great passion: fishing, loving nothing better than to spend the day on the grassy banks of the stream near their home with a fishing rod in his hands and a jam-jar of worms beside him.

When he did catch a fish it was generally too small and he would throw it back with a smile; he enjoyed the experience more than the result – until Voetsek started chasing butterflies and barking at every bird or beetle that dared to come near them.

'You can't come with me unless you behave,' he said to Voetsek, and the dog licked his hand to indicate he understood.

They settled at Jabulani's favourite spot just below the footbridge, where the stream formed a deep pool under the willows before winding its way through the valley.

Jabulani sat back against the knotted trunk of a tree, holding the rod given to him by the old Indian fisherman who had taught him to fish, while Voetsek lay next to him with his head on his paws, apparently asleep but alert to any intruding butterfly or bird.

Jabulani thought about the football team and about the big match that would be played the following weekend against a rival school. He was an intelligent boy and, because his parents had always encouraged him to think for himself, he did well at school, but had one great shortcoming: he was unbelievably clumsy.

He wanted desperately to play football for his school team, but always fell over his own feet. 'You have bad co-ordination,' the team coach had said to him one day in frustration, 'you will never be able to play football.'

Jabulani was devastated; he thought it was a disease and for days he wondered what medicine he could take to cure it. When he discovered in the dictionary that it simply meant various parts of his body 'did not work or act together', he was so relieved he went around telling everybody happily, as if it were a blessing, that he had bad co-ordination.

A large, yellow butterfly with black dots fluttered over the nearby reeds and Voetsek, unable to resist the temptation, leaped up, barking frantically, and chased after it before Jabulani could stop him.

He splashed along the shallows and leaped high to catch it, but in vain, for it fluttered away across the stream. Jabulani watched him sternly: 'You said you would behave,' he scolded. 'Now you've frightened away any fish that may have been interested.'

Voetsek crept back with his tail between his legs and lay a little distance away, watching Jabulani with large, soulful eyes. 'And it's no good feeling sorry for yourself, I'm not impressed.' Jabulani cast the line out into the middle of the pool pretending to be angry and Voetsek gave a little whimper of apology.

Just then Jabulani saw a large shape glide towards his float and the wriggling worm at the end of his hook and he stood cautiously. 'Don't move,' he whispered and Voetsek went rigid, 'not a sound, keep absolutely still.'

Jabulani had never seen such a beautiful fish, or such a large one, in his stream. It was all the colours of the rainbow and shimmered like the sequins on his mother's evening dress. 'Oh, what a magnificent fish,' he gasped. 'I can't bear to catch it, I'll pull out the line.'

But as he spoke, the fish, which had been circling slowly, decided to swallow the tempting morsel; the large mouth closed like a vice on the bait, and the fish was well and truly hooked.

As the barbed hook pierced the tender flesh inside its mouth, the fish reacted rather violently; it arched its back and leaped into the air, splashing and wriggling, then it churned through the water, tugging at the taut line that held it in thrall.

This was all too much for Voetsek who ran around in circles, barking frantically. Suddenly the fish stopped threshing and lay quite still, suspended in the clear waters of the pool. Jabulani laid the rod on the grass so he could attend to the fish and a deep voice echoed across the water: 'Set me free at once!'

Jabulani looked across at the opposite bank, but there was nobody there; he looked around and on all sides of him, but still could not discern anybody.

'Who said that?' he asked loudly, but got no response. Voetsek had stopped barking and was growling, his eyes fixed on the water. 'You heard something too, didn't you?' Jabulani said, turning to the dog.

'You were mean to use that nice, juicy worm as bait. Please set me free,' the voice echoed across the water once again.

Jabulani looked at the fish lying quite still in the pool; its large, unblinking eyes were fixed on him and the pouting mouth opened and closed with the fishing line stretching from one side of it.

'I must be going crazy,' he said. 'There's nobody else here, only this fish.' Voetsek barked in agreement and then growled again.

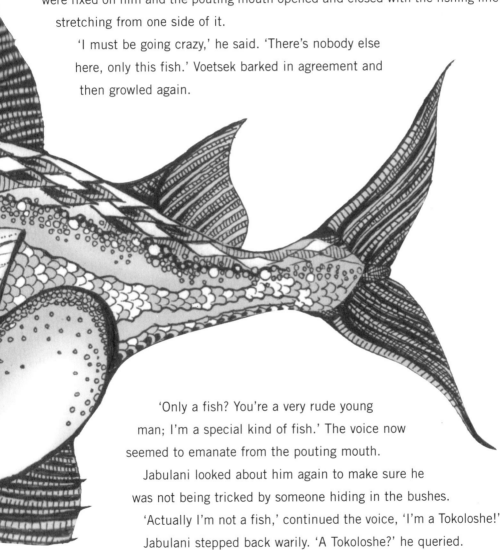

'Only a fish? You're a very rude young man; I'm a special kind of fish.' The voice now seemed to emanate from the pouting mouth.

Jabulani looked about him again to make sure he was not being tricked by someone hiding in the bushes.

'Actually I'm not a fish,' continued the voice, 'I'm a Tokoloshe!'

Jabulani stepped back warily. 'A Tokoloshe?' he queried.

'Of course! Tokoloshes can take any shape they please,' said the creature,' and this morning a fish shape took my fancy. Now look at the tragic consequences.'

'Are you really a Tokoloshe?' asked Jabulani. 'I can't believe it.'

The fish moved impatiently: 'You really are a most disbelieving young man,' it said. 'Just set me free and I'll prove it to you.'

Jabulani knelt down and took up the line, then paused. 'The things I've heard about the Tokoloshe are not good,' he said. 'People say you are wicked and evil.'

'Spiteful tongues,' said the Tokoloshe-fish. 'I just like a little fun, that's all. Set me free and I'll prove it to you.'

Jabulani turned to Voetsek, who was still growling softly. 'What should I do?' he asked. 'Should I set him free?'

Voetsek barked defiantly, making his feelings quite clear.

'If you do,' said the fish, 'I'll do anything you ask, I have very special powers, I can make your dearest wish come true.'

Jabulani smiled. 'I was going to set you free anyway,' he said, 'but now that I know you're a Tokoloshe I'll probably regret it.'

He reached out and drew in the line with the fish, which remained passive and inscrutable, took the smooth head with its gleaming scales firmly in one hand and gently eased the hook from the tender flesh.

As he drew the barbed hook out of its mouth, an amazing happening occurred; the water around the fish seemed to swirl like a vast whirlpool and a flickering light illuminated the fish, which gradually started changing shape; the gleaming scales became soft fur, the fins became hairy legs and arms and the fishy eyes and mouth became a monkey face with bright eyes and a small, flat nose.

Then there was a flash and a splash and suddenly a little Tokoloshe creature was bounding and leaping about on the bank shouting, 'Free! Free! Free!'

Voetsek chased after him barking frantically, at which the Tokoloshe pointed a bony finger at the dog: 'Stop that idiotic barking,' he said and from the tip of his finger pulsed a bluish energy, like an electric current, which seemed to envelop Voetsek who immediately became mute; his mouth opened and closed but no sound came out.

'What have you done?' asked Jabulani in alarm, as Voetsek slunk to him completely demoralized by his inability to bark.

'Just a temporary measure to restore our hearing and our sanity,' said the impish little creature. 'He was getting on my Tokoloshe nerves.'

'But he feels inadequate without his bark,' said Jabulani. 'Please allow him to bark again.'

'I'll do better than that,' said Tokoloshe, 'I'll let him speak,' and he pointed his finger again. This time there was a reddish light that enveloped Voetsek and suddenly he said, in a gruff voice, 'Just let me get my teeth into his fur, I'll teach him a lesson.'

Jabulani couldn't believe his ears. 'Voetsek, you can speak,' he said in amazement.

'I've been speaking for years,' said Voetsek, 'only you haven't bothered to listen. I could understand you without any difficulty.'

Tokoloshe broke into a chattering laugh; he was squatting on his haunches like a monkey and rolled over backwards as he laughed. Jabulani studied him with interest. 'I've heard you can make yourself invisible,' he said. 'Is that true?'

Tokoloshe sat up. 'Of course it's true,' he said proudly, 'it's one of my best tricks,' and he rolled over with laughter again. 'You should see the mischief I get up to when I'm invisible.'

'I wonder if he's a monkey,' thought Voetsek, as he lay with his head between his paws, watching.

'Mischief?' said Jabulani. 'What do you do?'

'Well,' said Tokoloshe, 'all manner of things. I turn myself into a river crab and nip the toes of the maidens when they bathe in the stream.' He chattered with laughter again. 'I put thorns under the old ladies when they sit down; you should see them leap up, Aai! Aai! Aai!' And he almost choked with laughter at the thought.

'I think that's just childish,' said Jabulani. 'How do you become invisible?'

SOMETHING FISHY

'Childish?' said Tokoloshe indignantly, 'it takes great skill.' He reached into a leather bag that hung around his neck and pulled out a small pebble about the size of a pullet's egg. 'I have this magic pebble and when I rub it I disappear. First I'm here then, pouf, I disappear!'

Jabulani was sceptical. 'If you can disappear, he said, 'show me.'

'All right, I will,' said Tokoloshe and he took the smooth, round pebble and rubbed it as he chanted: 'Pebble of the Tokoloshe, please hear and make me disappear.' Then he jumped high in the air, clapped his hands and squatted on his haunches.

'There,' he said, 'I'm invisible.'

Jabulani laughed. 'Invisible?' he said scornfully. 'You're still here, I can see you!'

Tokoloshe shook his head pityingly. 'I have many ways of being invisible,' he said, 'and this is one of them. You can see me, but nobody else can; to everyone else I'm invisible.'

Jabulani laughed. 'What nonsense,' he said, 'I don't believe you.'

At that moment a group of boys, members of the school football team, togged up in their football gear, crossed the bridge on the way to their practice.

At the sight of Jabulani they stopped. 'Hey, it's Jabulani,' shouted one of them. 'What have you caught today, Jabulani?'

The others laughed. 'He couldn't catch his own mongrel,' shouted another and they all chanted in unison, 'he's got bad co-ordination,' and roared with laughter.

Jabulani glanced at Tokoloshe who was waving and jumping up and down. 'It's true,' he whispered in astonishment, 'they can't see you.'

'Watch out the sharks don't bite,' shouted one as they started moving off.

Over the years, Jabulani had got used to their taunts, especially from Samson who was the team captain and the school bully to boot, so it didn't bother him and he ignored them. But Voetsek was bristling with indignation and shouted: 'You're just a bunch of idiots who couldn't even catch a cold if you tried to,' and added, as the boys turned back, 'you don't have the brains to do anything but chase a ball around all day.'

Samson moved to the front. 'What did you say?' he shouted. 'If you want a hiding you're really asking for one.'

'No, no, it was a mistake,' called Jabulani, adding under his breath, 'shut up, Voetsek, you'll only get me into more trouble.'

'Come on,' called one of the boys, 'we'll be late for the practice,' and the others pulled Samson away.

'The next time we meet I'll teach you some manners,' he called as they moved off along the path.

'Now look what you've done,' said Jabulani, turning to Voetsek, 'now you've got me into real trouble. I liked you better when you couldn't speak.'

Tokoloshe rolled over, chattering with laughter. 'Well,' he said, sitting up, 'that's settled that. Now tell me, what do you want me to do?'

Jabulani was confused. 'What do I want you to do?' he asked. 'What do you mean?'

Tokoloshe sighed and rolled his eyes. 'I gave you my word that I would do whatever you desired,' he said, 'and a Tokoloshe is always true to his word.'

Jabulani scratched his head. 'I don't know,' he said. 'I suppose the only thing I really want is to play for the school football team.'

'Then you shall play for the team,' said the impish Tokoloshe, 'and I hope you don't mind if I have some fun getting you there.'

'What do you mean "fun"?' asked Jabulani warily.

'Never mind,' laughed Tokoloshe, 'that's my secret,' and he leaped into the stream. 'See you at the football match,' he called as he bounded and splashed under the bridge and disappeared up the stream, chattering and laughing.

'Now I know he's a monkey,' said Voetsek.

'Oh be quiet, Voetsek,' said Jabulani irritably, 'and one more thing, don't you dare say one word while we're at home. You've got me into enough trouble already.'

'I won't say another word or bark another bark,' said Voetsek sulkily.

Jabulani laughed, 'Only to me.' he said, patting Voetsek, 'but not to others, promise?'

Voetsek nodded happily. He was pleased to be friends again.

A week passed during which one significant event occurred in Jabulani's life; his name appeared on the notice board, listed as a reserve for Saturday's match. The coach couldn't remember how or why he had decided to include Jabulani but, as it was only as a reserve, he wasn't overly concerned.

Jabulani was pleased to be listed as a reserve, even though he was disappointed not to be in the team and he decided that Tokoloshe had done as much as he could.

The day of the match dawned and Voetsek couldn't understand why Jabulani was so excited. 'They're going to chase a ball around for hours and you want to join them,' he said incredulously.

Jabulani tried to explain about competing and about ball skills but Voetsek was not convinced. 'Well, I hope the monkey keeps his word, that's all I can say,' he said as Jabulani left and he settled down to wait for his return.

In the changing room the boys ignored him, laughing and joking among themselves, but just before the start of the match Samson came across to him. 'I don't know how you even managed to get in as a reserve,' he said grimly, 'but it makes no difference. I'll see you after the match.'

Jabulani took his place on the reserve bench and suddenly Tokoloshe was sitting beside him. 'Don't worry, they can't see me,' said Tokoloshe grinning broadly. 'Are you ready for the fun?'

There was a roar from the crowd as the match started and immediately Samson dribbled the ball skilfully past two defenders. 'What fun?' asked Jabulani, turning to Tokoloshe, but he was no longer there, he had disappeared completely.

Samson raced towards the goal with only the goalkeeper to beat. The crowd were on their feet as he unleashed a drive towards the top corner of the goal. The ball sped straight and true, but at the last moment swerved violently and flew over the bar. The crowd became silent and Samson stood frozen in disbelief – he had never missed from that range before.

That was only the first of several inexplicable lapses from Samson. On one occasion he made to tap the ball back to his goalkeeper, only to see the ball rocket into the net for an own goal. On another occasion, with the opposition goalkeeper entirely at his mercy again, he tripped as he was about to kick the ball and fell flat on his face.

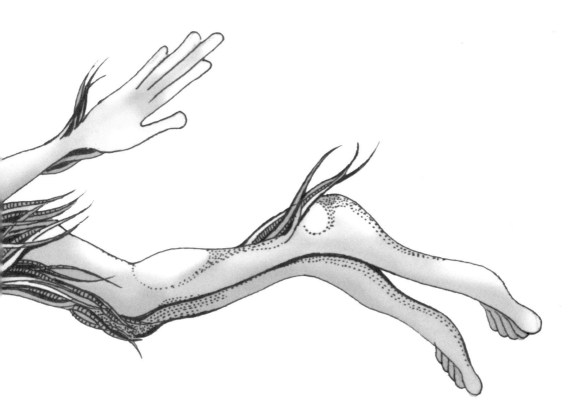

Some of the more fickle members of the crowd started booing whenever he had the ball; it was an entirely new experience for Samson.

Jabulani watched in amazement. He knew that Tokoloshe had something to do with what was happening but, in spite of Samson's arrogance, Jabulani felt sorry for him.

Half-time arrived and so did Tokoloshe beside him. 'What have you done?' asked Jabulani. 'That was all your doing, wasn't it?'

'There's more to come,' said the mischievous sprite and before Jabulani could say any more, he disappeared again.

Then the coach came up to Jabulani. 'You're on,' he said grimly. 'I've taken Samson off; you couldn't be any worse than he was.'

Jabulani was very tense as he walked towards the field. Suddenly Tokoloshe was walking beside him. 'You're on your own now,' he said encouragingly, 'show them what you can do.'

'But I need your help,' said Jabulani desperately, 'don't leave me now.'

'I'll be there when you need me,' said Tokoloshe, 'just believe in yourself,' and with that he disappeared.

The score was 2-1 in favour of the visiting team and without Samson the home team seemed set for defeat, but Jabulani had something to prove, to himself as well as the team, and suddenly he wasn't clumsy anymore; he felt Tokoloshe beside him and his confidence soared.

The two goals his team needed to win came within minutes; the first when Jabulani saw a high cross from the far touchline floating across the goalmouth. His feet seemed to grow wings as he flew through the air and headed the ball into the far corner amidst pandemonium from the supporters.

The second goal came when he burst free and dribbled around two defenders before unleashing a drive, which rocketed into the net like a bullet. The final whistle sounded amidst scenes of jubilation as Jabulani was borne off the field shoulder-high.

There was great rejoicing at the victory and, after all the back-slapping and congratulations were over, the rest of the team trooped off to celebrate and Jabulani was left alone in the change-room.

Suddenly Tokoloshe was sitting next to him with his infectious grin. 'That was fun, wasn't it?' he said.

'Thank you for helping me to score those goals,' said Jabulani. 'I could never have done it without your help.'

'Oh, I didn't do anything,' said Tokoloshe, 'it's true I had a hand and a foot in the first half, but after that it was all your own doing.' He jumped up with a laugh: 'And now I've granted your wish, I'm free to go,' and he took his magic pebble out of its bag, 'and when I go, your dog will stop speaking and make dog noises again.'

'My own doing?' said Jabulani in wonder.

'Yes,' said Tokoloshe. 'You just needed to believe in yourself, that's all,' and then he rubbed his magic pebble and was gone in a flash and a shimmer of light.

Jabulani moved slowly to the door and then stopped. In the passageway Samson stood waiting for him. Jabulani braced himself as Samson moved slowly towards him and the two of them stood face to face. Then Samson smiled and held out his hand. 'Not bad,' he said, 'not bad at all.'

Coming from Samson that was high praise indeed.

THE GOOD TOKOLOSHE
AND THE EVIL TOKOLOSHE

Tokoloshe sat with his back against the smooth rock-face at the base of the waterfall. The tumbling water cascaded over the edge of the cliff high above him, thundering and sparkling as it fell, creating a shimmering curtain before him.

Although the main force of the water missed him, the spray drenched him, plastering and matting the fur on his head and body. Tokoloshe stuck out his tongue and channelled a rivulet of water into his mouth.

This was one of his favourite spots. The dark pool swirled before him in the shadow of the cliff and sparkled brightly as it sped into the sunlight, past the large, flat rock where he sometimes sunned himself, and then lost its way as it meandered through the valleys and rocky ravines.

He grinned happily and the grin creased his face from pointed ear to pointed ear. The world was quite different seen through a curtain of cascading water; the liquid sun undulated, staining the sky with streaks of crimson; the trees danced and waved their branches at him; his own face peered at him from the watery mirror.

His own face? There were pointed ears and a small, flat nose set in a furry face, but the eyes were glaring balefully at him. They were not his eyes!

Tokoloshe sprang to his feet and the face disappeared. He darted through the curtain of water into the churning pool beyond, but there was no sign of the face or its owner. He dived deep into the pool and his sharp eyes scanned the depths, but there was nothing, nobody!

He arrowed to the surface, emerging like a sleek gannet after its dive, then froze in astonishment, for sitting casually on *his* rock, with knees drawn up under its chin, was his mirror image!

Tokoloshe was so outraged he froze motionless above the surface of the pool, for Tokoloshes are able to stand and glide on the water. Then he leaped onto the rock and crouched before the creature who gazed at him impassively.

'Who are you?' he asked, 'and what are you doing here?'

The other Tokoloshe curled his lip. 'My name,' he hissed, 'is Nyoka, and I can strike like a mamba.' Tokoloshe was not intimidated. 'What are you doing in my pool?' he asked. 'On my rock?'

The stranger's eyes glittered. 'Now it's my pool too,' he sneered, 'and my rock!' Then he sprang to his feet and faced Tokoloshe. 'My waterfall, my stream, my reeds! Mine! Mine! Mine!' he screamed.

Tokoloshe was speechless. 'How dare this upstart, this poor imitation of a Tokoloshe who called himself Nyoka, trespass on his territory?' he thought. 'And have the impudence to claim it was his, too?' But before he could give vent to his outrage, Nyoka disappeared. He had become invisible.

Tokoloshe frantically rubbed his magic pebble and in a trice was also invisible, for it is another fact of Tokoloshe lore that invisible Tokoloshes can see one another.

But, however thoroughly he scoured the pool and the stream for a kilometre upstream and down, there was neither hide nor hair of Nyoka.

Tokoloshe was somewhat unsettled. More than that, he was deeply troubled. Never before had he encountered such a vicious and disagreeable Tokoloshe. He had come across many other Tokoloshes who commanded different stretches of the stream and they delighted in recounting their pranks and mischief to one another, but it was an unspoken rule that Tokoloshes only ventured into one another's territory respectfully, observing due decorum.

Never, ever had he been challenged with such impudence! 'Go away and stay away,' he shouted across the pool and his voice echoed down the valleys and ravines.

Tokoloshe decided he needed some diversion to dispel the memory of that unpleasant encounter. He had begun to feel a new emotion, hatred, and it was an emotion he didn't like very much. It was as if that evil creature had transmitted some of its malevolence to him.

He decided to join his friends, the young boys of the village, in their favourite pastime, swinging out over the river on a monkey-rope and bombing one another in the water. They always had great fun, yelling and taunting one another as they launched themselves at the bobbing heads below.

Mandla was a particular favourite of Tokoloshe. He was smaller than the other boys and one of his legs was twisted from an accident at birth, so he walked with a limp and had to endure the teasing his name provoked.

'Please don't hurt us,' they would laugh cruelly, 'you are so strong and powerful, Mandla,' and they would yell with laughter. He kept much to himself, but had a wicked sense of humour – which drew Tokoloshe to him – and Mandla would roll about with laughter at Tokoloshe's accounts of his latest pranks or escapades.

This particular morning he was sitting alone, watching the other boys splashing and taunting one another, when Tokoloshe joined him and they sat side by side watching the antics.

'Come on,' said Tokoloshe, 'let's show them how to make a really big splash, like hippos when they dive,' and he grabbed Mandla and pulled him towards the monkey-rope. 'You go first and I'll follow.'

Mandla grabbed hold of the vine. 'Just don't fall on top of me,' he laughed. Then he swung out over the stream, stretching his legs to increase the momentum of the swing, and as he swung back he made himself into a tight ball.

Tokoloshe ran with Mandla on the second swing and gave a vigorous push, which launched Mandla high into the air. He soared above the bobbing heads below and then plummeted into the pool with a mighty splash, screaming with excitement and delight.

Tokoloshe followed him and the boys cheered and waved as he flew through the air higher and higher because, of course, Tokoloshes can soar as high as they want. Then he fell to earth like a meteor and a huge plume of water, higher than the tallest tree, rose on his impact.

He shot to the surface, brimming with laughter and looking to share his joy with Mandla, but his friend was nowhere to be seen. Then he realized the boys were yelling and pointing to the spot where Mandla had disappeared.

He plunged into the depths, anxiously scanning the muddy bottom of the stream. He saw a figure at the deepest part of the pool and streaked towards it, but as he got near he realized it wasn't Mandla but the Tokoloshe who called himself Nyoka!

Nyoka's face was contorted with hatred and he was holding a limp figure that was struggling feebly to free itself. It was Mandla! A surge of intense energy and anger powered Tokoloshe, who launched himself at the hateful creature, cannoning into him with the force of an explosion, blasting him backwards and releasing the figure of Mandla, who flailed upwards to reach the surface and air for his bursting lungs.

The two Tokoloshes faced each other with anger and hatred flowing between them. 'I'll destroy you and your friends,' hissed Nyoka, 'my master has instructed me!'

Tokoloshe felt a wave of anger engulf him and an almost uncontrollable desire to attack and destroy this foul monster, but he forced himself to remain calm, for he knew that they were equally matched in strength and power and the only way to overcome Nyoka was to outsmart him.

'You're full of threats,' he laughed scornfully, 'but you always run away when I face you. You disappear like a cowardly hyena.'

Nyoka was overcome with fury and the water around him boiled and bubbled. 'We'll fight now,' he screamed. 'I'll destroy you! I'll cut you into little pieces!' He held his tail before him like a sword; it ended in a lethal barb and was now glowing and pulsing with energy.

'And you're afraid of facing me openly in case the boys see you being beaten,' taunted Tokoloshe.

Nyoka was beside himself. 'Come on,' he screamed, 'let's fight in front of them,' and he launched himself like a fiery projectile out of the pool and onto the grassy verge, where the boys scattered as he appeared. Tokoloshe followed him and they faced each other again, surrounded by the astonished boys.

Mandla was sitting with his back against the roots of a mangrove tree, recovering from his ordeal.

'Whoever is beaten leaves this stream and never returns,' said Tokoloshe, 'and, remember, a Tokoloshe is bound by his word!'

'Agreed,' sneered Nyoka. 'Say goodbye to your stream.'

The boys formed a circle around them: 'It's a fight.' The whisper spread like wildfire and a wave of excitement came over them, for boys understood the law of the jungle; the law of survival where the strongest prevailed.

Tokoloshe stood nonchalantly grinning and swinging his tail, for he knew his only hope lay in provoking Nyoka into such a fury that he would lose control and that would affect his judgment. Tokoloshe's eyes were sharp and his mind was alert to any eventuality as he stood, idly swinging his tail.

Overcome with fury at this display of nonchalance, Nyoka launched himself at Tokoloshe with a scream, lashing his lethal tail like a whip, but Tokoloshe was alert and ready and at the last moment he leaped up, grabbing the monkey-rope and swinging high as Nyoka flashed past beneath him.

The boys cheered and leaped about with excitement at Tokoloshe's clever ruse and Nyoka turned furiously to face his adversary again. His charge had taken him close to the tree where Mandla was now crouching and with a triumphant shout he grabbed the boy and pulled him up, but Mandla was ready for him this time and gathered a handful of sand and flung it with all his might into Nyoka's face.

With a howl of anger and frustration, Nyoka released Mandla and clutched at his face. At that moment Tokoloshe, swinging back, cannoned into him and the hapless creature was thrown against the tree with such explosive force that the earth seemed to shake. In a groaning heap he fell at the foot of the tree and Tokoloshe immediately released his hold on the monkey-rope and dropped like a lead weight onto the writhing figure. The impact winded Nyoka completely and he lay inert, gasping for breath.

The boys cheered again and, lifting Mandla onto their shoulders, closed in on the two combatants.

Tokoloshe squatted on Nyoka's back and lashed him across the legs with his own tail, which was still glowing and pulsing fiercely. 'Do you surrender?' he demanded as he lashed the helpless creature.

'Yes, yes,' gasped Nyoka, 'please don't beat me anymore!'

'And you will keep your promise to leave us in peace?' continued Tokoloshe, beating him again. 'Yes, yes, I will! Please stop,' screamed Nyoka.

Tokoloshe jumped up and the boys drew back as the battered and bruised Nyoka slowly got up. 'I'll go,' he muttered, 'but it's the end of me, my master does not tolerate failure, and I have failed.'

Tokoloshe drew close to him. 'That depends on you,' he whispered in his ear. 'You can break his power if you really want to.'

The little creature, who was no longer looking malevolent but rather troubled and even puzzled, rubbed the pebble hanging around his neck. 'Farewell,' he said. 'Do you really believe I can break free from his power?' But before Tokoloshe could answer, he disappeared in a hum and a pulse of energy.

The boys crowded around Tokoloshe and Mandla – they had witnessed a fight that they would never forget.

In a dark and dank hut, festooned with the skins and bladders of small animals, crouched an obese, old man. His body and his bulging belly were daubed with ochre and on his shaven head he wore the beaded headdress of the *Sangoma* or *Inyanga*.

He was muttering and chanting before a circle he had traced in the dust and on which he had thrown a handful of small bones. 'Itsi! Itsi! Itsi!'. He sneezed three times to cleanse his spirit, then took up the bones once more and rocked on his haunches.

His eyes and his face bore the same malevolent expression that had been etched on the face of Nyoka. He was not pleased with what he had seen in the bones, and his belly and chins quivered with indignation. He threw the bones into the circle again and leaned forward to study them.

Then an amazing thing happened! The bones started flashing and fizzling like sparklers. The old man started back in consternation. The sparks flew in the air all about him; some fell on the grass thatch of the hut, which started smouldering and smoking. Then tongues of flame leaped up and soon the hut was ablaze. The old man leaped to his feet with amazing agility for his size and ducked through the low entrance into the open air.

As he did so, the face of Nyoka appeared in the smoke and flames, but it was no longer malevolent. Now a mischievous grin creased it and his eyes sparkled and he laughed with a chattering, monkey laugh.

He had become a free spirit once again.

HOW THE TORTOISE GOT ITS SHELL

In the beginning, it was said, Tokoloshes inhabited every stream, waterfall and pool in Africa. It was also said that, at first, they were just gleamings of energy that flickered and danced on the waters.

What wasn't said, though, was that there were other forms of energy that shared the streams with them. These were quite different, because where the Tokoloshes were fleeting and swift, these were slow and somnolent, like large, soft jellyfish floating on the water.

But the Tokoloshes got on very well with them, for they constantly changed shape as they squished and squashed themselves, tumbling along on the water. Moreover, they gleamed with a greenish glow, unlike the Tokoloshes who flickered with a blue or white radiance.

You may be wondering where these other beings came from, for, like Tokoloshes, they were beings who could play games and have fun.

The answer to your wondering lies in the stars, for these beings were life forms that had travelled across space, swifter than a moonbeam glancing off the water, and when they reached Earth they found kindred spirits in the streams and in the pools and waterfalls of Africa.

Now it happened that when the Tokoloshes decided to become small, hairy creatures, not unlike monkeys, the globules of energy (for they had no name then) wondered what shape they could take to avoid detection, for they had also become aware of the danger posed by the big ones of Earth.

Finally, after much soul-searching, they decided to revert to the shape they had been on their distant planet; small, pale beings with large heads and eyes, but with spidery arms and legs. They called themselves 'Extra Terrestrials', ETs for short, for they had come to earth from outer space.

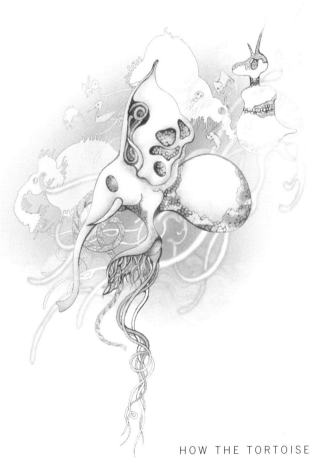

When the Tokoloshes first saw these pale, spidery beings with large heads and saucer-shaped eyes, they rolled about with laughter; they chattered and gasped with glee; they tumbled about in paroxysms of mirth.

The ETs were bemused, they looked at each other in astonishment, they couldn't understand what the Tokoloshes found so funny. Then one of the Tokoloshes led an ET by the hand to the edge of the stream and pointed with his bony finger at the reflection in the water and, unable to contain himself any longer, doubled up with mirth and plunged head-first into the stream, spluttering and choking with laughter.

At this, one of the ETs led a Tokoloshe to the edge of the stream and pointed at the monkey face, hairy body and knobbly fingers and toes that were reflected in the water and all the ETs opened their mouths wide and shook with silent laughter.

Finally, one of the Tokoloshes said: 'You can't go about looking like that. You look...,' he was about to say 'weird,' and then he remembered that he himself looked remarkably like a monkey and he ended up saying lamely, 'unusual'.

The leader of the ETs, who had larger eyes than the others, approached him and spoke in a soft, gentle voice: 'We may be unusual here on earth, but this is how we appear in our own world.' Tokoloshe squatted before him and the ET leader suddenly shrunk to his size, 'We have a mission here on earth,' he said in the same gentle voice. 'We have to report regularly to our planet about the big ones,' he sighed sadly, 'and about the weapons they invent. You see, on our planet, weapons are forbidden and war is unknown.'

Tokoloshe nodded, he could understand that. 'But don't you see,' he said, 'with your present appearance they will find you easily, they will put you in cages, they will treat you like they treat their animals.'

The ET leader looked distressed and the other ETs started weeping large, silent tears, for they had seen animals in zoos and in cages. 'But what other shape can we take to be safe?' he asked. Tokoloshe thought at length: 'That will take all my Tokoloshe ingenuity.' And then, as if to explain the word 'ingenuity', he added, 'We have to be clever and tricksy,' and he chattered with laughter and splashed into the stream. 'I will dream an answer for you tonight,' he said, 'and tell you in the morning.' Then he chattered with laughter again and disappeared up the stream.

Next day, at dawn, all the ETs gathered near the large pool below the willows; they gleamed like pale, green lanterns in the morning gloom – hundreds of lanterns, reflected magically in the dark waters of the pool. They stood silently, waiting for the Tokoloshe who would dream them a form.

The sun rose, at first just a flush on the cheek of night and then later as a blood-red ball, appearing slowly, inch by inch, until it rose clear of the horizon and flooded the world with light. Still the ETs stood silently; their large eyes mirrored the awakening day.

Suddenly there was a chattering and a splashing as Tokoloshe appeared around the bend in the stream; he stopped in astonishment at the sight of such a multitude gathered around the pool. As he moved to the centre of the pool, the ETs followed and surrounded him. They parted for their leader who addressed Tokoloshe: 'Have you dreamed a shape for us?' he asked.

'Well,' replied Tokoloshe mischievously, 'when I closed my eyes, I dreamed of river-food and in my dreams I had such a feast that I felt sleepy.' He paused dramatically and then added, 'but you see, I was already asleep,' and he gurgled with laughter.

The ETs stood silently, watching and listening. 'Yes,' said the leader, 'and then?'

Tokoloshe wiped his eyes. 'And then,' he said, 'I dreamed of some extra-special mischief.' He paused and, as there was no response from the ETs, he sighed. 'Actually,' he said, 'I dreamed a form for you.'

'Yes?' said the leader. 'What is it?'

HOW THE TORTOISE GOT ITS SHELL

Tokoloshe grinned his cheeky grin. 'In my dream,' he said, 'I asked myself three questions: How can you become inconspicuous? Where can you hide when there is danger? And what can you do to appear harmless?'

'And did you dream the answers to those questions?' asked the ET leader.

'Of course I did,' said Tokoloshe indignantly. 'I never wake up before my dreams are finished.'

'And what answers did you dream?' asked the leader with infinite patience. 'How do we become inconspicuous?'

Tokoloshe grinned smugly. 'The big ones won't notice you if you are slow and placid,' he said. 'In fact, they won't notice you at all if you are as slow as you can possibly be.'

The ET leader nodded. 'I understand,' he said, 'they are always rushing everywhere. And where can we hide when there is danger?'

Tokoloshe rolled his eyes. 'Obviously you need some armour,' he said, 'some protection wherever you go, and I have devised the perfect armour to protect you.'

He pointed a bony finger at the nearest ET and, under a pulsing and a flickering flow of energy that emanated from his fingertips, a strange transformation took place. The ET's spidery body slowly became covered with a hard carapace, so that just his head and his arms and legs protruded, and then the weight of the carapace forced him onto his hands and knees.

The assembled ETs drew back with a collective gasp, for what they saw was a long neck and head protruding from a shell that moved as slowly as a snail; the head had the same bony ET shape with large, unblinking eyes.

The ETs clapped their hands slowly and soundlessly until Tokoloshe held up his hand. 'And the final question,' he said, 'what can you do to appear harmless? No problem, just be timid and eat only plants,' at which the transformed ET withdrew into his shell and disappeared from sight. Tokoloshe chattered with laughter and splashed in the water with delight.

The ET leader held up his hand. 'You have given us our salvation,' he said in his gentle voice, 'from henceforth each of us will become...,' he paused and looked down at the shell and at the little head that was just appearing, '...a tortoise. That will be our name – tortoise – because you "taught us" how to survive.'

So they all grew shells and moved off ever so slowly to the far reaches of the planet and if anyone asks you how the tortoise got its shell you can tell them and then whisper, 'It's really an Extra Terrestrial in disguise.'

They probably won't believe you, but it doesn't matter, because you know the truth, don't you?

HOW THE BEE GOT ITS STING

It was a hive of activity as the bees buzzed to and from their hive and it made Tokoloshe feel quite dizzy just watching them. 'Buzz, buzz, buzz,' he said, 'honey, honey, honey,' for Tokoloshe understood the language of the bees. 'Just like the big ones,' he thought, 'only with them it's "buzz, buzz, buzz, money, money, money".'

The big ones had found the right word for the industrious, little insect, he mused. *Isanuzi* sounded just like the busy, buzzing bee.

He squatted in the shade of his spreading fig tree, patiently watching the bees at their toil, gathering nectar from the flowers to make their honey. His observation, however, was not motivated by an interest in the daily life of the bee. He had a less altruistic motive than that: he wanted their honey.

The beehive was situated in the hollow bole of a knotted tree nearby, known as a *Spathodia* or Flame Tree, because it bore flame-coloured flowers. However, the bees were far more interested in the fields nearby, where daisies and phlox flowered in profusion.

Tokoloshe was waiting for the light to fade and the activity to diminish before he made his move. His plan was simple; he would creep up to the tree, quickly thrust his hand into the hollow bole and come away with a handful of honeycomb dripping with the sweet, sticky, delicious honey.

As he waited, the thought of the golden nectar became more and more irresistible, until he could contain himself no longer and he got up and crept towards the tree. There seemed to be little or no activity around the hive and Tokoloshe was tired of waiting, so he thrust his hand into the hollow, feeling the sticky honeycomb beneath his fingers and, as swiftly as a mamba strikes, he broke off a large piece, withdrew his hand, turned and fled.

But swift as he was, he wasn't swift enough, for a swarm of angry bees pursued him, buzzing ferociously. Through the trees he streaked, followed by the angry swarm.

'Ow! Ow! Ow!' Tokoloshe yelled and leaped about as the bees dived and attacked him, stinging him on his arms, his legs and his bottom. He reached the stream and dived in, all thought of the honey having disappeared. The bees buzzed about angrily for some time, while Tokoloshe lay at the bottom of the stream, feeling acutely the stinging pain the bees had inflicted on him. Finally, they decided to return to the hive, leaving their victim covered in bumps and without any honey, for he had dropped the honeycomb in his flight.

Tokoloshe emerged cautiously from the stream and, when he was sure the bees had disappeared, sat on the bank and started squeezing and pinching the stings from the lumps on his arms and legs; his bottom was more difficult and he twisted and turned, whimpering and feeling very sorry for himself.

Finally, when he had removed all the stings, he plucked some leaves from a nearby bush, which he knew had medicinal properties, and rubbed them on the lumps. Soon the pain and the swelling diminished.

But he was not a creature to bear a grudge; he accepted the stings and arrows of outrageous fortune as readily as he subjected others to his pranks and mischief. In fact, he soon saw the funny side of what had happened and his grin returned as he pictured himself leaping about and yelling 'Ow! Ow!'.

The incident awakened his insatiable curiosity; he wondered how it was that the bees had acquired such potent stings.

Suddenly he thought of the most outrageous idea. It was the sort of idea that sent frissons up and down his spine, that made him shiver with excitement and expectation; he would change himself into a bee; he would become Isanuzi and enter the hive, to find out how the bee had acquired its sting.

Immediately he rubbed his magic pebble and in his invisible state he crept up to the hive again. There were one or two straggler bees who were the last to return with their nectar and their pollen sacs full and Tokoloshe at once made himself the size of a bee and squeezed inside the last one, who buzzed loudly and described a circle in the air as she did so. In his new persona Tokoloshe entered the hive for one of his most unusual adventures ever.

Inside was like a palace with gleaming white walls of wax and passageways leading to countless, large, six-sided chambers where hundreds of bees were engaged in depositing their nectar.

Tokoloshe decided to become a dormant passenger and allowed his bee to take over, for she seemed to know exactly where to go and what to do. She headed for one of the hexagonal cells that was empty. 'Buzz, buzz, buzz,' she said to a neighbouring bee, 'late, late, Maya late.'

'Buzz, buzz, buzz,' responded the other bee, who had just completed offloading her nectar, 'honey, honey, honey.'

They were very repetitive, thought Tokoloshe, but at least they didn't indulge in pointless chatter and gossip like the big ones, only essentials: work and honey, and he had learned the name of his bee, Maya.

Tokoloshe started dozing off, for it was very warm and cosy in the hive, but he awoke with a start as Maya started moving. She had finished off-loading her honey and was now heading along one of the passageways. He wondered whether he should take over, but decided to see where she was headed.

They moved along numerous passages, passing cells where bees were either resting or sleeping after their long day's work; at one point they passed a much larger passage guarded by some aggressive bees. 'Buzz, buzz, buzz,' they buzzed, 'move along, move along, move along.' Tokoloshe wondered what lay at the end of that wide, well-guarded passage. Determined to find out, he abandoned his dormant role and took control.

Maya turned about sharply and headed back towards the large passageway. 'Buzz, buzz, buzz,' said Tokoloshe inside the bee, 'explore, explore, explore.'

When the sentry bees saw Maya approaching again they became even more aggressive, and several of them buzzed simultaneously. 'Buzz, buzz, buzz, go back,' buzzed one; 'no entry,' buzzed another; 'we will attack,' buzzed a third.

Tokoloshe saw their vicious-looking stings ready to inflict untold misery and decided it was time to reveal his true identity. 'Buzz, buzz, buzz, I am a Tokoloshe,' he said. 'My spirit has entered this worker bee and so I appear as one of you.'

Suddenly he had a flash of inspiration, for he remembered being told about the Queen Bee who governed each hive. 'I am here,' he said, 'to bring important tidings to your Queen.'

There were more words strung together in Tokoloshe's speech than the sentry bees had heard before and it confused them; they were only ever used to simple, direct language like 'work', 'honey', 'guard' and 'destroy'. They advanced menacingly towards Maya and their buzzing became a deafening roar. 'Buzz, buzz, buzz, Tokoloshe! Intruder! Destroy!'

Suddenly, as Tokoloshe was about to eject himself from the hapless bee he had inhabited, a deep droning sound reverberated throughout the hive and the sentry bees immediately prostrated themselves. The droning suddenly stopped. 'Buzzzzzz,' a husky voice whispered, 'bring the Tokoloshe before me.'

Tokoloshe realized the wax walls of the cells and passageways would conduct any sound for a considerable distance and they must have been overheard. The sentry bees were thrown into further confusion and started moving in circles. 'Buzz, buzz, buzz,' they were frantic, 'Majesty, intruder! Destroy!' and they started bumping into each other.

'Buzzzzzz! Bring him before me!' This time the voice was imperious. Maya, alias Tokoloshe, was ushered along the passageway, which broadened into a vast chamber of glistening, white walls. A group of worker bees were swarming about and attending to someone who could only be the Queen Bee.

Tokoloshe gaped in astonishment, for she was huge, so huge that she filled up half the chamber. Her little head seemed quite out of place on her huge, white body, which spread out behind her like a gross, white caterpillar, soft and convoluted.

'Buzzzzzz, are you a good Tokoloshe or an evil Tokoloshe?' Her husky voice jolted him out of his astonishment. 'Show yourself in your true form.'

Tokoloshe squeezed out of Maya and stood beside her in his diminished size, which was no bigger than a bee. 'I am not an evil Tokoloshe, Your Majesty,' he said, 'I like a little fun, that's all.'

'So you decided to steal some of our precious honey.' she whispered. 'Do you call that fun?'

For an instant Tokoloshe was speechless. How did the Queen know of his escapade? 'Well,' he stammered, 'I paid for it, didn't I? I was stung all over.'

'And did you know,' she continued, 'that every bee who attacked you, paid for it with her life?'

Tokoloshe was horrified. 'I didn't harm them,' he protested.

'No, but when a bee stings an enemy,' she whispered, 'her sting is ripped out of her body and she dies.'

Tokoloshe looked devastated.

'Every bee is prepared to die for her hive,' concluded the Queen, 'to ensure the survival of her Queen and her fellow bees.'

Tokoloshe hung his head in shame.

'Buzzzzzz, why have you come here in the guise of this foolish bee?' she continued relentlessly, pointing at Maya, who was struggling to understand everything that was being said.

'It was not her fault,' said Tokoloshe, 'she didn't have any choice. I just squeezed into her and took over.'

Maya gave him a grateful look; she was beginning to like this funny, little creature who had become part of her.

'Buzzzzzz, you haven't answered my question,' said the Queen sternly. 'Why have you come here?'

'Well, Your Majesty...,' Tokoloshe had intended to make up some impressive tale about new pesticides that could harm the bee colony, but under her level gaze he decided to tell the truth. 'When your bees stung me,' he paused, 'I'm sorry, I didn't know they died to protect their hive.'

The Queen remained silent.

'I wondered how and why they had acquired such a venomous sting and so I decided to find out,' he concluded lamely.

The Queen regarded him silently for some moments. 'Buzzzzzz, sit down and I'll tell you a story,' she said.

Tokoloshe perched on a large lump of wax and waited expectantly; he noticed the worker bees attending the Queen also settled down to listen.

'Buzzzzzz,' began the Queen, 'this same story has been told since bees first inhabited this world and it has been passed on from one hive to another.' She paused and took a sip of honey from a wax container beside her, then began to tell her story.

'Long, long ago, bees were no different from the flies that buzzed around and settled on anything, anywhere, causing irritation and aggravation. One such bee settled on a Tokoloshe, who was dozing idly in the sun and woke him up,' she paused and looked directly at Tokoloshe, 'he was an evil Tokoloshe.'

Tokoloshe jumped up, but before he could protest that not all Tokoloshes were evil, she held up her hand. 'Don't interrupt me,' she said imperiously, 'unless you wish to feel their stings again!'

Tokoloshe noticed the bees attending the Queen had adopted aggressive stances, so he sat back meekly on his wax seat. Maya moved closer to him: 'Buzz, buzz, buzz,' she whispered in his ear, 'do not speak, listen.'

Tokoloshe was impressed by her vocabulary, which appeared to be improving.

'He was an evil Tokoloshe,' repeated the Queen, 'and so he decided to punish the troublesome bee for bothering him and he gave her a sting.' She paused and indicated the worker bees about her, 'And he gave all the other female bees stings too, for he enjoyed the thought of them stinging other creatures and causing pain.'

The assembled bees started a soft, buzzing refrain, 'Buzz, buzz, buzz, evil, evil, evil,' which was unsettling to Tokoloshe.

'Silence!' commanded the Queen, and they instantly obeyed.

'Buzzzzzz, but he was even more malicious than that,' she whispered, 'for he decreed that when they used their stings, the stings would be torn from their bodies and the bees would die.'

Disregarding the risk of being stung, Tokoloshe stood up. 'Majesty, that was a terrible thing to do, but not all Tokoloshes are evil, in fact only a few of us are; most of us just love to have fun.'

He waited in dread for the expected tirade, but instead the Queen smiled. 'I asked you earlier whether you were a good Tokoloshe or an evil Tokoloshe,' she said, 'but you have interrupted and I haven't finished my story.' She paused and Tokoloshe sat down, 'However, this time we will forgive your indiscretion.'

'Silly, silly, Toko,' whispered Maya, and she buzzed with laughter.

'One day, another Tokoloshe,' the Queen paused significantly and then added, 'it was a good Tokoloshe this time, was threatened by a bee. "Why do you want to sting me?" he asked, and the bee could think of no answer except, "because there's nothing else to do", adding, "and I'm bored".

'"Well, I'll give you something to do," said the Tokoloshe sternly, "and you'll be so busy doing it, you won't have time to think about yourself." Then he showed her the flowers, and when she tasted their nectar she became instantly addicted.' The Queen paused and turned to her attendant bees. 'Who can finish the story?' she asked.

There was great consternation and buzzing amongst the bees for they had never been asked such a thing before and most of them could only repeat a few words. Then Maya stepped forward. 'Buzz, buzz, buzz,' she said, 'Toko teach bees to make wax.' The Queen nodded. 'That's right, Maya,' she said.

'Buzz, buzz, buzz, Toko teach bees to make hive,' Maya was now into her stride. 'Buzz, buzz, buzz, Toko make Queen to rule.' The other bees buzzed in agreement, 'Buzz, buzz, buzz.'

Maya was now in a state of great excitement. 'And, and, and...'

'Calm down, Maya,' said the Queen, 'you will buzz yourself into a frenzy.'

'Buzz, buzz, buzz,' Maya buzzed more calmly, 'and Toko make bees to move pollen,' she continued, 'from flower to flower to make seeds.' It was the longest sentence she had ever spoken and it quite exhausted her.

The other bees buzzed loudly, which Tokoloshe took to be their way of clapping.

'Buzzzzzz, thank you, Maya,' said the Queen. 'At least one of my ladies has some common sense.'

She turned to Tokoloshe, who had been held spellbound by the story. 'So you see, Tokoloshe, your good Tokoloshe gave us bees a mission in life; he gave us all these things, and,' she added mischievously, 'he gave us honey to feed our young...,' she paused, '...which you tried to steal.'

Tokoloshe stood up. 'Your Majesty,' he said with a grin, 'a leopard cannot change its spots and a Tokoloshe cannot stop having fun,' adding with a wink, 'or stop making mischief.'

'Buzzzzzz,' the Queen was shaking as she buzzed and Tokoloshe realized she was laughing. Then she said, 'I am tired now and need some rest.' At once her attendants buzzed around her in concern, 'Maya will escort you from the hive.'

'Thank you, Your Majesty,' said Tokoloshe, 'for telling me how the bee got its sting,' and he moved to Maya who was waiting for him in the passageway, 'and how the bee got its honey,' and he couldn't resist adding, 'I'll think twice before stealing honey again.'

'Buzz, buzz, buzz,' Maya nudged him, 'cheeky, cheeky, Toko,' she said.

'Yes I am, aren't I?' he said happily. 'Now let's ride piggy-back,' and he leaped onto her furry back and held on tightly under her wings.

Maya didn't need a second invitation for she was determined to give him the ride of his life; she zoomed down the passageways like a rocket and emerged from the hive into the bright sunlight, then dived and looped, while Tokoloshe clung like a limpet until finally she settled on a branch of his favourite fig tree.

'Wheee, that was fun,' exclaimed Tokoloshe, hopping off her back and onto the branch.

'Buzz, buzz, buzz, fun, fun, fun,' repeated Maya.

Tokoloshe had grown quite fond of the funny little bee, 'I'll visit you again,' he said.

But Maya grew sad and he saw a little tear in the corner of her eye.

'Not another one,' he thought. 'Whenever I make a friend, it causes sadness.'

'Buzz, buzz, buzz,' Maya buzzed sadly, 'Queen will soon leave hive.' She was struggling with her emotions, 'Buzz, buzz, buzz, new queen will come. Maya will go with old Queen.'

Tokoloshe was astonished. 'Why will your Queen leave the hive?' he asked.

Maya was silent, then she buzzed softly, 'Buzz, buzz, buzz, new queen fly high, only strongest drone bee can reach her.' She paused again and another tear fell on the branch, 'Together they rule new colony.'

'And you will leave with the old Queen,' said Tokoloshe, understanding that the world kept changing for all creatures, except Tokoloshes.

Maya nodded, then brightened and buzzed on a happier note: 'Buzz, buzz, buzz, Maya have present for Toko,' and Tokoloshe saw she had left a wax container filled with honey on the branch.

'I will visit you soon,' said Tokoloshe, 'for more honey.'

'Buzz, buzz, buzz,' said Maya as she flew away, 'cheeky, cheeky, Toko.'

And Tokoloshe wondered if he would ever see her again.

HOW THE GOAT BECAME SURE-FOOTED

Imbuzikazi the goat was ugly; there is no other word to describe him. He had small, yellow eyes that could glint meanly if he felt so inclined; he had a long jaw with bristles and a white, straggly beard that made him look like one of the seven dwarves, the one named 'Grumpy'. He also had a pair of curved horns, and woe betide anyone who got on the wrong side of him. He would lower his head and charge and, when he butted, he usually left a large bruise, or worse.

To add to this litany of ills, there was one that transcended all the others; he was stubborn. The word 'stubborn' seems inadequate to describe Imbuzikazi, for when he decided to do something, or not do something, nothing in the world would make him change his mind. He was so stubborn he developed the habit of doing exactly the opposite of what he was asked or told to do.

His owner, who was an old goatherd almost as ugly and almost as stubborn as Imbuzikazi, soon developed a strategy to counter Imbuzikazi's stubbornness. If he wanted Imbuzikazi to move, he would tell him to lie down. In fact, he told him to do exactly the opposite of what he wanted and it always worked.

On the day our story starts, Imbuzikazi was grazing high in the hills, above the stream that wound like a silver ribbon through the valley below. He was careful to

keep well away from the edge of the cliff
that fell away sheer to the stream below, and
where only eagles and buzzards nested or
perched with impunity.

Like all goats at that time, Imbuzikazi was nervous of
heights and the thought of his little hooves slipping on the
smooth stone made him uneasy.

But on that day he felt unusually contented as he
munched at the tender shoots and felt the warm sun
caress his matted fur and, as he chewed, his beard
waggled and he looked for all
the world as if he were
talking to the trees and
the tall grass.

Suddenly, his contentment was disrupted by the sight of a small, furry creature chattering and leaping about in the tall grass near the edge of the cliff.

It was Tokoloshe, of course, who had decided to scale the cliff so he could get a view of his stream from above. When he reached the summit and saw the wonder of the valley and his stream below him, he was so overjoyed that he started tumbling and cartwheeling with delight.

When his excitement had abated, he squatted right on the edge of the cliff and surveyed the panorama below, for Tokoloshes have no fear of heights and can walk straight up the face of any cliff.

He could see for several kilometres upstream, as far as the waterfall that glistened in the distance, and downstream he could make out the little footbridge that spanned the stream just below the willow-pond. From that height the world looked like a miniature one for tiny beings and Tokoloshe chattered with delight at the thought.

Suddenly he was rudely jolted out of his reverie by a bump and a thump on his bottom, which sent him hurtling over the edge of the cliff and cartwheeling into space.

Being a Tokoloshe, he was able to arrest his rapid descent and when he found a convenient ledge he perched on it for a few minutes, rubbing his bottom, which was really quite sore.

When he had recovered sufficiently, he started walking slowly up the face of the cliff, resting once or twice on convenient ledges before reaching the summit.

When he climbed over the edge of the cliff the first thing he saw was Imbuzikazi, munching away at the grass. He moved warily towards the goat and when he was a few feet away he stopped and said: 'Did you do that?'

Imbuzikazi lifted his head and regarded the little creature before him. Seldom had he seen anything so ugly, he thought: no beard, no horns and a face like a monkey's.

'Did you butt me?' said Tokoloshe angrily, again rubbing his bottom, which was now throbbing quite painfully.

Imbuzikazi was a goat of few words, so he lowered his head and charged at the little creature again. This time Tokoloshe was ready for him and leaped up high, allowing Imbuzikazi to pass beneath him.

'It looks as if you need a lesson,' said Tokoloshe tersely, pointing a bony finger at the goat. The energy that flickered from his fingertip seemed to envelop Imbuzikazi like a wave and it lifted him high in the air. Moving beneath the goat, he twirled his finger and the goat started spinning like a top above him. Then Tokoloshe walked down the face of the cliff, still with Imbuzikazi suspended in the air, and deposited him on a narrow ledge halfway down the cliff.

'There, you can stay on that ledge for a few hours, until you've cooled down,' Tokoloshe said with a grin before moving away to resume his enjoyment of the view, uninterrupted by the troublesome goat.

Imbuzikazi stood on the ledge, not quite understanding how he had got there. He moved forward cautiously; the ledge was narrow but his little hooves seemed to traverse it like a tightrope walker, carefully but surely.

Suddenly he felt elated. 'This is fun,' he thought and, without stopping to consider the risk, leaped towards another ledge, which was a little higher and even narrower. He landed surely and paused to look at the view. 'Wheeee! This is the best fun I've had for a long time,' he said to himself, and leaped towards another ledge.

And so, at times picking his way carefully foot by foot and at times leaping nimbly from ledge to ledge and rock to rock, he made his way to the top, arriving in a state of exhilaration.

Tokoloshe was squatting at the edge of the cliff with his eyes closed, for he had dozed off in the warm sun.

Imbuzikazi considered what he should do next; the urge to butt this hairy creature was overwhelming, but his recent exhilarating experience was somehow related to this creature, so he didn't. Instead he nudged him gently with his horn.

In a trice Tokoloshe was wide awake and faced the ugly goat. 'How did you get off that ledge?' he demanded. 'You should still be there.'

Imbuzikazi curled his lips and showed his teeth, which in goat language is a smile, but Tokoloshe jumped away. 'Are you at it again?' he demanded. 'Now you want to bite me! Haven't you learned your lesson?'

Imbuzikazi, as we have said, was a goat of few words, but he decided that this was the time for a few. 'Follow me,' he said and turned towards the edge of the cliff.

Tokoloshe followed him, quite perplexed by the goat's behaviour.

Imbuzikazi leaped nimbly from rock to rock and then made a mighty leap down towards a ledge tight against the face of the cliff. 'Are you coming?' he called to Tokoloshe, 'or are you too scared?' It was more than he had uttered for years, but he felt quite daring and adventurous.

Of course the challenge was too much for Tokoloshe. 'Scared?' he said in outrage. 'A Tokoloshe is never scared,' and he leaped onto the ledge beside Imbuzikazi. 'Go where you please and I'll follow,' he said.

And so they spent the rest of the day leaping from boulder to boulder, jumping across ravines and negotiating the narrowest ledges you can imagine and, finally, when they both lay in the long grass, exhausted from the adventures they had shared, Tokoloshe said, 'I have to admit I've had more fun today than I've had for a long time.'

Imbuzikazi curled his lips and showed his yellow teeth and this time Tokoloshe knew he was smiling.

In no time at all Imbuzikazi had convinced all the other goats that climbing cliffs and mountains where others couldn't venture was the best thing in the world and soon all the goats became sure-footed mountain goats.

In some countries the goat-herds have to tie bells around the necks of their goats so they can hear them and find them when they climb up into the mountains for some fun.

So, if anyone is described as being 'as sure-footed as a mountain goat' you'll know exactly what it means, won't you?

THE POISONED STREAM

His tummy was full and his mind was empty – or perhaps just vacant! He had gorged himself on sweet river-food, which he obtained by using his magical Tokoloshe powers. When he concentrated really hard on the food he wanted, and smelled it and tasted it in his Tokoloshe imagination, it magically materialized.

His first course had been an *hors d'oeuvre* – river mushrooms garnished with watercress. For his main course, he had visualized *waterblommetjiebredie,* a delicious stew made from the petals of water lilies – he had two helpings and burped loudly after the second. And for dessert he enjoyed a juicy watermelon, flavoured with chunks of root-ginger.

He lay drowsing on his flat rock, warmed by the afternoon sun, with his tummy as round as a football – and for a Tokoloshe that was very round.

He dangled his hairy feet with their knobbly toes in the stream and trailed his bony fingers where the water lapped around the warm rock. A dragonfly hovered above him and buzzed, 'Toko-Toko-Tokoloshe,' and he waved it dreamily on its way.

As he drowsed the afternoon away with vacant enjoyment, a strange thing happened: a large, cream-coloured water lily, with perfectly formed petals and long, golden stamens, floated towards him as if powered by an invisible force. As it

reached him it stopped, then began spinning like a top, emitting a low humming sound. As it spun, the petals curled down and opened out, leaving the stamens to form a perfect, golden crown.

At the sound of the humming, Tokoloshe's eyes flickered open and then, as the golden crown spun into his view, he leaped up as if galvanized by an electric shock, because every Tokoloshe knows that a golden crown spinning and humming on the water signifies a summons from the King of the Tokoloshes.

Tokoloshe danced a little jig of excitement on the flat rock as innumerable thoughts flashed through his head: the King of the Tokoloshes wanted to see him! What could it mean? Perhaps His Royal Majesty had heard of his latest escapade – after all, not every Tokoloshe gets to change into a cow or a bee!

Perhaps he was going to be congratulated royally, or perhaps even have the Royal Order of Tokoloshes, First Class, bestowed on him for his outstanding mischief. There was no time to lose; he had to set off right away!

He streaked into the stream like a moonbeam glancing off the water; sometimes he skimmed on the surface and sometimes he glided below like a shadow. And so he travelled for a day and a night, passing many small creatures who marvelled at his speed.

He passed a small, green frog who croaked, 'Toko-Toko-Tokoloshe,' as he whooshed by, and he passed a cheeky river-trout who bubbled, 'Toko-Toko-Tokoloshe,' as it glided out of his path, and he passed many other creatures of the river whose eyes opened wide in astonishment at the speeding tokoloshe, until finally he reached the deep, dark pool where the King of the Tokoloshes lived.

The King was resting on a ledge high against the stone face of the cliffs which surrounded the pool like a horseshoe. He lay in the mottled sunlight filtering through the tangled branches that reached out over the edge of the cliff high above him, feeling the warmth of the sun on his scales.

For the King of the Tokoloshes didn't look like a Tokoloshe; he looked like a large – a very large – lizard; in fact, he looked like a leguaan! He looked like a large reptile in every respect except one, and that was the golden crown tipped at a rakish angle on his horny head. He was humming a tune and then burst into song in a rasping voice: 'There's a rainbow on the river...'

He broke off and sighed: 'I do wish I could sing in tune! It's the tragedy of my life! I love music, but do you think it loves me? Whenever I try to sing, the notes just lose themselves in my head somewhere.'

He closed his eyes and swished his long, gleaming tail in the water. The King of the Tokoloshes had acquired the habit of talking to himself – not because it was an eccentric aberration, but rather the result of many years of enjoying his own company.

Tokoloshe approached carefully and knelt on the ledge below the King, coughed respectfully and waited.

The King of the Tokoloshes opened one large, yellow eye and regarded him balefully: 'Well?' he said. 'What do you want?'

Tokoloshe was confused. 'You summoned me, Your Majesty,' he stammered.

'Summoned you?' He opened the other eye. 'Of course, you're the Tokoloshe from...' he held up one scaly paw, '...no, don't prompt me,' he said, 'from the dam near the bridge. How's your dam and how's your bridge?'

'No, Your Majesty,' retorted Tokoloshe, 'from the pool near the willows.'

The King was not at all fazed by his lapse. 'Of course, the pool near the willows,' he said. 'Recognised you right away! Nothing wrong with the old memory, hey?'

Tokoloshe waited respectfully and, just when he thought the King had fallen asleep again, he continued, 'I summoned you because I have something to show you. Follow me!'

He slithered off the ledge and disappeared into a crevice that Tokoloshe had not noticed before. Tokoloshe followed him and the crevice opened into a large cavern, with ghostly, white stalactites reaching down from the darkness above. The sound of dripping water echoed eerily as the drops detached themselves from the gleaming tips of the stalactites and fell into the translucent waters of the large pool that covered the floor of the cavern.

When Tokoloshe's eyes became accustomed to the darkness, he saw the King of the Tokoloshes was now reclining on a throne of white limestone at the far end of the pool. A shaft of light from an aperture high above fell on a large globe that seemed to be suspended above the water.

Tokoloshe knew at once it was the magical crystal ball made of dragonfly wings in which the King of the Tokoloshes could see all manner of things, from the past and into the future.

'Look into my crystal ball,' said the King, 'and tell me what you sssssee.' He hissed the last word through his forked tongue, which flickered out as he spoke.

Tokoloshe approached the ball cautiously and peered into it. Through the shifting mists of the crystal ball he saw a scene that made his blood run cold and he recoiled in horror.

He recognised the stream some distance beyond his pool, but it was covered with dirty, green foam and slime; the shrubs bordering the stream had withered; the mossy banks had shrivelled and died; and the skeletons of fish and river crabs littered the banks. He recoiled at the stench that drifted from the mists of the crystal ball.

'What has happened?' he cried in anguish. 'Why has our sparkling stream become a sewer?'

The King of the Tokoloshes turned to the magical globe and whispered: 'Show us what has caused this disaster.'

The mists in the globe swirled and then slowly cleared, revealing a pipe that protruded from the bank of the stream and out of which gushed a thick, green liquid. It discoloured the clear waters of the stream, creating bubbling foam, which spread over it, covering and clinging to everything like glue.

'There is the poison,' hissed the Tokoloshe King. 'Your task is to find the perpetrator of this heinous crime and to put a stop to this deadly pollution.'

Tokoloshe turned to him in astonishment. 'My task?' he echoed.

'Yesssss,' replied the King. 'I have taken note of your escapades; you are resourceful and adventurous, not to mention mischievous and impertinent; you have the true qualities of a Tokoloshe and I have decided to entrust you with this quest.'

Tokoloshe glowed with pride. 'I will do my best, Your Majesty,' he responded. 'I will save our stream.'

The King nosed the ball of dragonfly wings, which floated out of the shaft of sunlight and disappeared in the darkness above.

'Well, get on with it,' he said, 'no point in hanging about like a lounge-lizard. Get to work.' That said, he coiled his tail around his head, closed his large, yellow eyes and was soon snorting loudly, which is what leguaans do instead of snoring.

Tokoloshe knew the interview was over and decided to leave at once. He was fired with a passionate desire to fulfil his destiny as a Tokoloshe and he streaked through the crevice and into the stream in one mighty dive, determined to solve the mystery of the poisoned stream.

Jacobus Christof du Plessis sat behind an executive desk and smoked an executive cigar. He was pleased with life, he was pleased with his lot, but most of all he was pleased with himself. His close friends called him Dups, but at the office and among his business associates he liked to be called J.C. because it reminded him of the Almighty, and he felt totally in control.

J.C. was a loving man at heart; he loved his two Rottweilers, he loved his two kids and he loved his wife, in that order. If he had one failing it was Greed, with a capital G.

As a child, little Dups had lived with a hard, unrelenting God; his father was frequently out of work and, therefore, frequently drunk. His mother believed the only way to instil respect was with a strap and so little Dups suffered many painful lashings and was told that God was punishing him. He never really understood why.

When he graduated from little Dups to J.C. he had learned some hard lessons; the first was to look after Number One, because nobody else would. The second was to grab anything worthwhile that came his way, before somebody else did, because in this life it was a case of 'dog eat dog'! And something really worthwhile had come J.C.'s way.

He had heard that Solly Rabinowitz was in trouble, deep financial trouble.

Solly was the owner of a small tanning factory, situated above the bridge spanning the steam that flowed through the town. His factory had been broken into and the thieves had made off with almost the entire stock of hides that had been hanging to cure. About seventy valuable hides had been stolen and foolishly, or perhaps carelessly, Solly was not insured.

Through his past dealings with some of the more 'shady' characters in the district, J.C. suspected who was behind the robbery and made an offer to purchase hides, with no questions asked, at a ridiculously low price.

The upshot of his acumen and astute grasp of the situation was that J.C. now owned the factory, bought for a 'song' from Solly Rabinowitz, and with it a stock of valuable hides. So J.C. had good cause to be pleased.

His reverie was interrupted by a knock on the office door. Before he could respond, the door opened and in came Petrus. J.C. had tried to make him understand that he should wait until he was instructed to enter, but Petrus either didn't understand, or didn't want to.

He stood nodding and smiling and shifting from one leg to the other. He had worked for Solly Rabinowitz for twenty years and knew all there was to know about curing hides.

'Yes, Petrus, what is it?' he asked. Petrus smiled and nodded: 'The tank she is full,' he said, as if he were bringing glad tidings.

J.C. could never understand how Petrus distinguished between the masculine and feminine genders and he didn't try to work it out.

'All right, Petrus, I'll attend to it,' he said. 'Just close the valve and leave the skins in the *muthi* tonight.' Petrus looked worried, so J.C. added: 'You've worked hard today, take the rest of the afternoon off.' Petrus stood uncertainly. 'Go on, go home,' ordered J.C. brusquely and Petrus withdrew, shaking his head.

When J.C. took over the business he had conducted a thorough evaluation and from the outset he had identified one of the major difficulties, which was the disposal of the tannic acid used to treat the hides. It was a highly toxic substance and when the hides were soaked in it they became soft and malleable, but the acid sludge had to be stored in a large tank, which had to be emptied regularly.

The disposal of the sludge – including the use of a tanker to pump it out – was a costly business.

J.C. had cast his eyes to the heavens for inspiration and had come up with an ingenious solution. He had paid a friend of his, a qualified plumber, to install an escape valve leading to an outlet pipe that terminated on the banks of the stream and, when the tank became full, he would open the valve at night and allow the acid sludge to drain into the stream.

Everyone believed he had disposed of the sludge legitimately and J.C. was pleased. He didn't care in the least about the stream or the fish and plants that were dying. 'Goggas and weeds, that's all they are,' he thought. 'Who cares about them?'

On the evening of our story, he phoned his wife to tell her he would be home a little late ('some unexpected business') and he enjoined her to keep his dinner warm. He calculated the drainage would take about two hours.

He lit another cigar, sat back in his executive chair and blew two perfect smoke-rings; he would enjoy his cigar and his thoughts for ten minutes and then get down to business.

He watched the two smoke-rings curling upwards and then a strange thing happened: one of the smoke-rings started changing shape and slowly turned into the skeleton of a fish, with sharp, pointed teeth.

J.C. sat up and rubbed his eyes, but it was still there; then the second smoke-ring became a crab with large, snapping pincers.

He stood up in alarm and consternation as the two phantom creatures turned to face him and started moving towards him with jaws and pincers snapping.

He leaped backwards, knocking over his chair and falling heavily on the polished floor; then he scrambled up and faced the two smoky apparitions, but all he saw were two smoke-rings slowly dissipating in the air.

He picked up the glowing cigar with a muttered oath: 'Must be something funny in this cigar,' he said, and ground it out in the large, ceramic ashtray on his desk. 'Maybe I've been working too hard,' he said to himself. 'Anyway, let's get down to work.'

He moved purposefully down the passage and opened the door to the curing-room, where dozens of hides were hanging from the drying racks.

As he walked between the racks towards the large tank that contained the tannic acid, the second strange thing happened: the hides on either side of him became alive and started slapping and lashing him.

J.C. yelled in alarm as one skin lashed him across the back and, as he turned, another slapped him in the face, and suddenly they were all gyrating and flapping and slapping him as he ran towards the tank.

As he reached the tank, he received a mighty lash, which sent him sprawling and he banged his head heavily against the base of the tank. He sat up with a groan and raised his arms to protect himself from further punishment, but all he saw were rows of hides hanging peacefully from the drying racks. He waited for a few minutes and, when nothing further untoward happened, got slowly to his feet.

J.C. did not understand what was happening to him, it was like a nightmare he could not shake off. Perhaps he needed a holiday, he thought, just *braais* with beer and *boerewors.* That would set him right.

At the back of the tank he unlocked a panel that concealed the secret escape valve and opened it, switched on the pump and watched the needle on the pressure-gauge start its gradual anti-clockwise movement towards zero. 'Two hours to get rid of all that muck,' he thought as he went back to his office.

And then the third strange thing happened. As he reached his office door, he felt the floor vibrating beneath him and a photograph of young Dups captaining his school rugby team, which had been hanging on the wall behind his desk, crashed to the floor in splinters. 'It must be an earthquake,' he thought in alarm, and clung to the door.

Back in the curing-room, Tokoloshe watched with satisfaction as the tank shuddered and juddered; it had been a simple task to close the escape valve and turn up the pump to full power, much simpler than his magic with the smoke-rings and animating the hides, which had required intense concentration.

But the result of this last act of mischief was awesome; an irresistible build-up of pressure within the tank, which sent the needle of the gauge well into the danger area. Something had to give and Tokoloshe watched the rivets on the steel covering of the tank pop out like popcorn, before the whole tank exploded in a fountain of sticky liquid.

Tokoloshe chattered with delight as the toxic stream burst through the door into the passage and flowed towards J.C., who was pinned against his office door in terror. At the last moment he managed to force the door open and, overcome with terror and desperation, ran across the room and dived through the window in a shower of glass, landing with a splash in the polluted stream below.

The final piece of Tokoloshe's plan fell into place when a live cable, ripped free by the exploding tank, sparked furiously as it coiled on the wet floor and soon the whole building was ablaze.

J.C. watched the tongues of flame leaping up into the sky and tears ran down his cheeks at the thought of how unfairly he had been treated by the Almighty; he had not even taken out an insurance policy.

Tokoloshe sat before a circle of small skeletons he had arranged on the bank of the stream and hummed a requiem for the dead fish; his humming seemed to envelop the stream and lap against the banks, purifying the skeletons; it echoed and resonated across the still waters and all the water creatures that were still alive stopped to listen and felt renewed.

CROCODILE TEARS

Tokoloshe was bored. He was so bored he was even bored with being bored. He had tried all his usual tricks, but found them all tedious; tickling toes or putting thorns on seats or shongololos in beds, the results were all so predictable. He put up his legs and wiggled his toes; he was wedged in the fork of his favourite fig tree and surveyed the world from a height.

What he needed was a new adventure, he thought, something really startling, something even more astounding than – he stopped, than what? He couldn't even remember his last adventure! How boring!

He sat up; he would visit his friend Mandla. Together they should be able to think of some daring exploit. He leaped down from the tree and made for the monkey-rope above the stream where the boys usually played but there was nobody there. Then he sped to the pool under the willows, where Mandla sometimes sat reading those strange sheets of paper with squiggles, but he wasn't there either.

There was only one thing for it; he would have to visit him at his home. He didn't like going too near the big ones, even if they were Mandla's parents, they still acted and thought as big ones and that was dangerous.

He rubbed his magic pebble that caused him to become invisible and was about to set off for Mandla's home when he saw a figure in the distance limping towards him; it was Mandla. In a trice he was beside him. 'I was just on my way to visit you,' he said.

Mandla stopped and looked about. 'Tokoloshe? Where are you?' he asked. 'Make yourself visible.'

'Sorry,' said Tokoloshe happily, and he rubbed his magic pebble again and slowly materialized.

The two of them sat side by side under the willow near the pool. 'We are going away,' said Mandla. 'The school has closed because there is much trouble in the land.' He turned away so that Tokoloshe should not see the tears that were forming in his eyes. 'My father is taking us to my uncle who lives in Mthunzini.' He stopped, unable to continue.

'When will you come back?' asked Tokoloshe blithely.

'Never,' whispered Mandla, 'we are going to live with my uncle.'

'Never?' repeated Tokoloshe puzzled. It was a word he didn't understand.

'Never,' repeated Mandla sadly. 'We will never see each other again,' and he started sobbing.

Tokoloshe got up and moved away. He was feeling a strange pain that he didn't understand and it was because Mandla had told him they would never see each other again. Then he remembered what the King of the Tokoloshes had once said to him. 'A Tokoloshe,' he'd said, 'must always be alone, to have fun and to enjoy making mischief. If he makes a friend, sooner or later they will have to part and he will start feeling sadness – that is not good for a Tokoloshe, for he will start becoming human.'

Tokoloshe turned on Mandla angrily. 'Why do you go with them?' he demanded. 'Stay here with me.'

Mandla smiled through his tears. 'I can't,' he said, 'I have to go with them, they are my parents.'

Tokoloshe didn't understand what that meant because he had no parents. He frowned and then suddenly his face was wreathed in a wide grin. 'I will go with you,' he said. 'It is time for a new adventure.'

'With me?' said Mandla, his face lighting up. 'How?'

'Oh, not for always,' said Tokoloshe, 'just for an adventure,' and he jumped up. 'I have heard of this shady place which the big ones call Mthunzini.' He performed a cartwheel and then squatted before Mandla. 'I have also heard of Ngwenya, the big crocodile who rules the river at Mthunzini,' he said. 'We will visit him and pay our respects.'

'How will you get there?' asked Mandla in wonder. 'You can't come with us.'

Tokoloshe wrinkled his nose. 'Have you forgotten I can be invisible?' he said loftily, adding, 'but I prefer to travel by water,' and he chattered with laughter. 'I'll get there before you,' and he bounded away towards his stream.

Mandla waved at the little form disappearing in the direction of the stream and wondered if he would see him again.

Tokoloshe knew that his stream flowed, after many kilometres, into a river and the river flowed for many more kilometres before reaching the sea. He had heard the big ones talk about the sea and he knew it was larger than the largest dam he had ever visited and the water in it had a nasty, salty taste.

He also knew that before the river reached the sea it formed a large dam that the big ones called a lagoon and that was the place called Mthunzini where Mandla and his parents were going.

He set off with a song in his heart and with his spirits soaring. He had started the day feeling bored, but now he was off on a great adventure and he was sure there would be opportunities for fun and mischief on the way.

Tokoloshe could travel fast in his stream; faster than the sunlight flickering through the leaves or a moonbeam glancing off the water, but this was an adventure so he was in no hurry. And, of course, he had to visit the other Tokoloshes and pay his respects when he passed through their territory, and they all wanted to hear about his latest escapades, for his tricks and his mischief had become well-known.

In this way the time passed swiftly and after three days he reached the point where his stream flowed into the wide river known as the Umlalazi. He stood in awe at the confluence of the two currents; he was quite at home in his little stream, even when the stream formed a large pool before continuing on its way, but he had never seen such a wide expanse of water flowing so swiftly before.

'Ooooooh!' His exclamation expressed his feelings of surprise and delight as he squatted and considered the next stage of his journey. He was excited at this new challenge; this was better than all the toes he had ever tickled; this was a real adventure.

He dived into the river and thrilled at once to the tug of the current as he looked about him. The fish were much larger and less friendly; one ugly fellow with a wide mouth came towards him aggressively, but quickly swerved away when Tokoloshe 'bopped' him on the nose with his little fist; then Tokoloshe did somersaults of delight in the water and laughed air-bubbles, which popped into chatters of laughter when they reached the surface.

For two days he travelled along the river and marvelled at the new sights he saw; river-weed that formed forests of softly swaying fronds, in which bright eyes glinted and then disappeared; once he tobogganed down a weir, over which the water rushed swiftly before churning around large boulders below.

He kept his sharp eyes peeled and his Tokoloshe senses alert for any sign of Ngwenya, but saw no sign of him.

At evening on the second day he reached the lagoon at Mthunzini and floated on his back, looking at the lights of the dwellings that twinkled through the mangroves growing profusely on the banks. Mandla would be staying in one of the dwellings near the lagoon, thought Tokoloshe, for he remembered Mandla had said his uncle worked for the Forestry and Nature Conservation Department. In the morning he would find him.

He made for a sandbank in the lagoon in the shape of a white horseshoe and slept soundly that night amongst the gulls and gannets also roosting there.

He was awakened bright and early by one of the gulls pecking at his feet; she had mistaken his knobbly toes for worms and was relishing the thought of a hearty breakfast. Tokoloshe shooed her away and sat up to greet the new day. He was feeling peckish himself, so he conjured up a juicy watermelon and gorged himself on it.

He gave a burp and the gulls squawked indignantly, then he rubbed his magic pebble and set off in his invisible state to find Mandla. He was confident of finding his friend without much trouble, for his Tokoloshe instinct was like an antenna that could 'home-in' on his target.

He passed the first few houses without feeling any vibrations, then decided to explore further along the lagoon where there were bungalows tucked in among the trees. As he passed the first bungalow his antennae started vibrating and he knew he was 'getting warm'; at the second bungalow the vibrations made him dizzy and he knew he had found Mandla.

He peered in through one of the windows and saw Mandla sitting at a table with his father and mother, having breakfast. He grinned and decided to have some fun.

Mandla had a bowl of mielie-meal porridge before him and was reaching for a jug of milk; suddenly the jug fell over, spilling the milk across the table. Mandla's mother looked up. 'Mandla, look what you've done!' she exclaimed. 'Fetch a cloth from the kitchen and bring some more milk.' Mandla stood up and, as he did so, his bowl of porridge fell to the floor with a crash.

His mother threw up her hands in exasperation. 'Now look what you've done,' she said. 'You really are the clumsiest child!' His father just shook his head and continued reading his newspaper. 'When you've cleaned up,' said his mother, 'there's a little more porridge in the pot.'

Mandla closed the kitchen door behind him and whispered: 'Tokoloshe, I know it's you, where are you?'

Tokoloshe grinned. 'Right behind you,' he said.

Mandla turned. 'When did you get here?' he whispered happily. 'I thought I'd never see you again.' There was no response and, after a pause, Mandla said uncertainly, 'Tokoloshe?'

'I'm not there any more; I'm sitting on the kitchen table now.'

Mandla turned again. 'I don't like it when I can't see you,' he said.

'Well, you'll just have to put up with it,' said Tokoloshe. 'It's too dangerous to appear here.'

At that moment the door opened and Mandla's mother came into the kitchen. 'Mandla, why did you close the door?' she said in surprise, 'and why are you talking to yourself?'

Tokoloshe grinned and stuck out his tongue at her.

'And why haven't you got the cloth?' She snatched the cloth from the sink. 'I have to do everything myself. Just get yourself more porridge,' she said and went out through the door angrily.

Mandla glared at the spot from which Tokoloshe had last spoken. 'This is all your fault,' he said.

Tokoloshe grinned cheerfully. 'Yes it is, isn't it?'

Mandla turned in frustration. 'And you're always moving about,' he muttered. 'I never know where you are.'

Tokoloshe chattered softly with laughter. 'Meet me at the lagoon when you've finished your breakfast,' he said. 'I'll be on the sandbank.'

'Mandla!' The father's voice was angry and Tokoloshe grinned as he watched Mandla scuttle through the door while he made for the lagoon to join the gulls and wait for his friend.

He soon dozed off in the warm morning sun and was awakened by a pebble that struck him a stinging blow on the arm; he leaped up with a yell and crouched low in alarm.

Standing on the far bank was Mandla, who immediately threw another pebble with great accuracy and it struck Tokoloshe on the leg. 'Serves you right,' yelled Mandla, 'for getting me into trouble.'

Tokoloshe picked up a shell that was lying at his feet and hurled it at Mandla and soon a hail of missiles was flying between them.

When they had exhausted the game, Tokoloshe went across the river and sat beside Mandla. 'I am going to seek Ngwenya, the large crocodile,' he said. 'Do you wish to come with me?'

'How can I come with you?' asked Mandla. 'You are going beneath the water.'

From around his neck Tokoloshe took a small bag which had been hanging next to his magic pebble. 'I have some seeds from the pawpaw tree that grows so high only birds or Tokoloshes can reach it,' he said.

He opened the bag and poured a pile of small, black pips into the palm of his hand. 'On this tree the pawpaws grow all year round.' He held out his hand: 'These pips are from one of the pawpaws I picked before I left.'

'Why did you bring them?' asked Mandla, mystified.

Tokoloshe grinned. 'If you swallow these pips,' he said, 'you'll be able to breathe underwater like me.'

Mandla shook his head apprehensively. 'This is Tokoloshe mischief,' he said. 'You are playing games.'

'If you are frightened to try it,' said Tokoloshe, 'you are not my friend.'

'Why should I be frightened?' said Mandla, holding out his hand for the pips. 'They cannot harm me, even if they don't work.'

'They will only work if you believe in them,' said Tokoloshe sternly, as he transferred the pips into Mandla's hand.

Mandla smiled and popped the pips into his mouth, chewed them and wrinkled his nose. 'They are bitter,' he said with his mouth full.

Tokoloshe leaped up and dived into the river. 'Come along,' he called as his head appeared above the water, 'let's visit Ngwenya.'

Mandla stood uncertainly. He had swallowed the pips, but didn't feel any different. 'No tricks,' he said and jumped into the river beside Tokoloshe.

'Now let us seek Ngwenya,' said Tokoloshe as they bobbed side by side. 'Come along,' and he disappeared beneath the water.

Mandla took a deep breath and dived down after Tokoloshe who was waiting for him on the sandy river-bed but, as Tokoloshe beckoned to him, he shook his head as he could feel his lungs starting to strain for air, and he pointed towards the surface.

Tokoloshe was at his side in an instant. 'Just breathe normally,' he said in Mandla's ear and his voice seemed to echo in the water.

Mandla shook his head frantically and tried to push up to the surface, but Tokoloshe held him firmly until, with his lungs bursting, Mandla opened his mouth and gulped in the water. It was the strangest sensation; instead of choking and drowning, the water was like a breath of fresh air that flooded into his lungs and relieved the pressure. 'I can breathe,' he said in amazement, 'I can breathe under the water.'

'Of course,' said Tokoloshe, 'didn't I say so?' His chattering laughter caused vibrations in the water. 'You have become like the fishes.'

'And I can speak,' said Mandla, and his voice echoed eerily in the depths.

'Come along,' said Tokoloshe, 'this is the beginning of another exciting adventure,' and they glided off side by side, hugging the sandy river-bed as they swam.

They spent the whole morning gliding and looping loops in the water, exploring forests of river-weed and playing 'catch' with the crabs. Mandla even tried to join Tokoloshe as he rode on the back of a large carp, but tumbled off as the carp wiggled in indignation.

They explored the river for many kilometres as it wound around the sand-dunes and gradually narrowed. Finally, they reached a point where a large tree-trunk had fallen across the river and Mandla stopped. 'I think we should go back,' he said, sitting down, 'my parents will expect me for lunch.'

Tokoloshe joined him on the tree-trunk. 'We'll search again tomorrow,' he said. 'Ngwenya must be around here somewhere.'

As he mentioned the great crocodile's name, an astounding thing happened: two large eyes suddenly appeared next to Tokoloshe and the log gave a mighty waggle, which sent both of them rolling in the mud.

'Did someone mention my name?' boomed a deep voice.

The two adventurers looked up and beheld a wondrous sight, for the log was in fact the great crocodile, awakened from his midday nap by being rudely sat upon!

Tokoloshe stepped forward and gazed in awe at the huge creature; its jaw was open, displaying rows of sharp and vicious-looking teeth, while its scaly body, which they had mistaken for a tree-trunk, snaked back for fully five metres.

'I am the Tokoloshe from the stream beyond the far mountains,' said Tokoloshe, 'and I have come to pay my respects.'

'A Tokoloshe?' Ngwenya gave a great sigh and the water became turbulent. 'I was a Tokoloshe once, too.'

'Why did you become Ngwenya, the great crocodile?' asked Tokoloshe curiously.

'Because I was tired of playing mean tricks,' said Ngwenya. 'I had so much more to offer.'

'But why did you become a crocodile?' asked Mandla, stepping forward.

Ngwenya turned his head and fixed his two large eyes on Mandla. 'Who's your little friend?' he asked Tokoloshe. 'He looks delicious.' He paused and blinked his eyes, 'I mean suspicious.' He nodded his head. 'Yes, that's what I mean, you look suspicious,' he said to Mandla.

Tokoloshe's eyes narrowed, but he said nothing.

'Well,' said Mandla, 'crocodiles are usually carnivorous.' He turned to Tokoloshe. 'That means they eat flesh,' he said in explanation.

'I know what it means,' said Tokoloshe, not taking his eyes off Ngwenya.

'That's exactly why I became a crocodile,' boomed Ngwenya, 'to show the world that we can be gentle and caring.' He smiled, but when he showed his teeth it was rather unsettling. 'Besides,' he said, 'I'm a vegetarian.'

Mandla was impressed. 'A vegetarian?' he said. 'That's wonderful.'

'I'm glad you think so,' said Ngwenya. 'I hate to see any creature suffer.' Two large tears welled up in his eyes.

Mandla was visibly moved.

'Won't you come into my cave?' said Ngwenya, indicating a dark recess in the river bank. 'I would like to show you my collection.'

A glint in Ngwenya's eyes when he said 'come into my cave' reminded Tokoloshe of an encounter he had once had with an evil Tokoloshe; it was a malevolent glint and it alarmed Tokoloshe.

'What do you collect?' asked Mandla.

'Objets d'art,' said Ngwenya grandiloquently, 'I am an art collector.'

'An art collector,' said Mandla, moving forward, but Tokoloshe stopped him. 'Perhaps some other time,' he said. 'We have to go now,' and he took Mandla by the hand.

Ngwenya moved with a sudden flurry and blocked their path, 'What's your taste?' He blinked again, and then said, 'I mean, what's your haste? Why are you in such a hurry?'

Tokoloshe realized that when Ngwenya corrected himself it was because the first word was generally what he meant – only he wanted people to think otherwise.

'Well, we don't want to be food...' Tokoloshe decided to play the same word-game. 'I mean rude,' he said. 'Yes, that's what I mean, we don't want to be rude, it's time to go.'

Ngwenya glared at Tokoloshe and this time even Mandla was aware of the malevolent glint in his eyes and backed away in fear.

Tokoloshe drew Mandla beside him, faced Ngwenya and pointed to the skeletons of fish and other river creatures that were scattered in front of the entrance. 'If you are a vegetarian,' he said sceptically, 'why is your cave littered with bones? You say you are caring and you even weep large tears, but everyone knows about crocodile tears.'

Ngwenya reared up with his jaws wide open, but Tokoloshe was unafraid. 'And you say you were once a Tokoloshe.' He shook his head sadly. 'I once met a Tokoloshe like you and he was an evil and a cruel creature. He was no longer a Tokoloshe.'

Ngwenya lunged forward, snorting furiously with his jaws open to devour the two of them, but Tokoloshe was ready for him and, quick as a flash, grasped a rusted iron stake he had seen earlier, lying in the mud, and thrust it into Ngwenya's mouth, jamming his jaws open.

As Ngwenya flailed and twisted in the water, attempting to free himself of the stake, Tokoloshe whispered to Mandla that it was his chance to escape. But Mandla was loath to leave Tokoloshe alone with the crocodile. 'What about you?' he asked anxiously.

'I'll see you back at the sandbank,' said Tokoloshe. 'Now go!'

Mandla swam off and Tokoloshe turned to face the furious crocodile. 'How can you call yourself a Tokoloshe?' he said. 'You are a disgrace; you are no better than the reptile you inhabit,' and having said that, he leaped onto the crocodile's neck and sat astride it as if he were at a rodeo.

Ngwenya turned and twisted, flailed and flapped, but could not dislodge the creature, who clung to him like a leech, whooping and whistling as the reptile churned about in the water.

Finally, when Ngwenya lay exhausted on the muddy river-bed, Tokoloshe climbed off his back. 'That was fun,' he said, 'but I have to go now,' and the bubbles of his chattering laughter left a trail in the water as he swam off to join Mandla on the sandbank, leaving the hapless crocodile to ruminate about verminous creatures such as the Tokoloshe.

The next day Tokoloshe and Mandla sat side by side on the river bank again; they had shared an adventure that would live forever in their memories, but it was now time to say goodbye. Tokoloshe had to return to his stream and, moreover, he had such tales to tell the King and the other Tokoloshes.

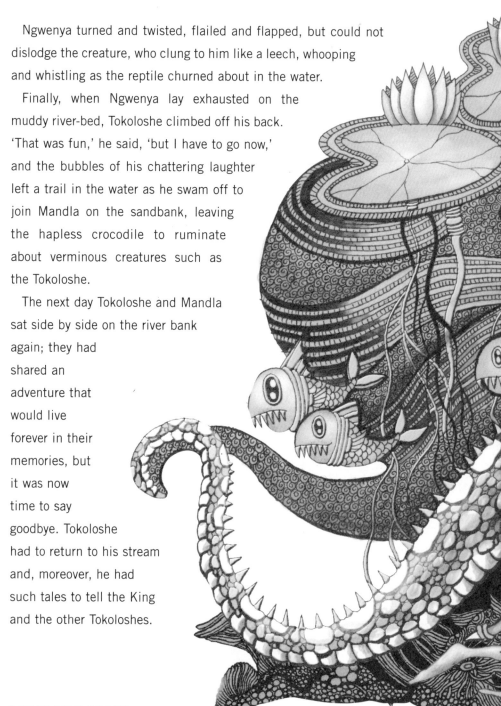

CROCODILE TEARS

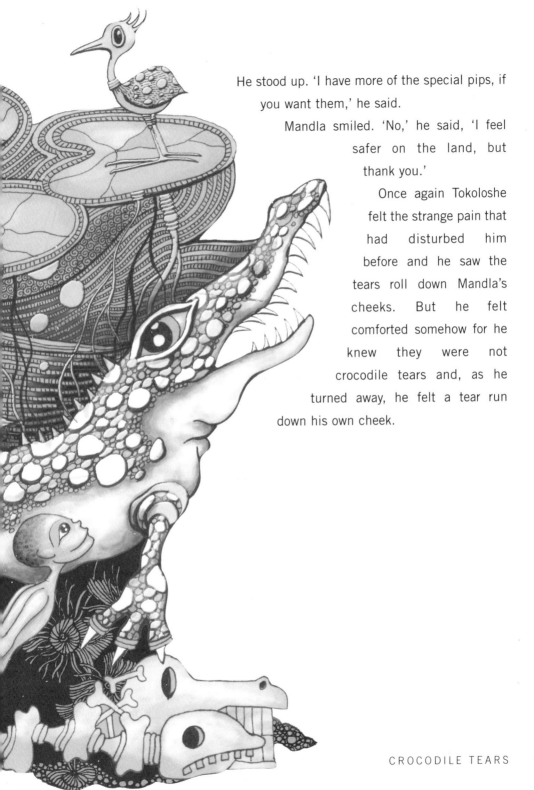

He stood up. 'I have more of the special pips, if you want them,' he said.

Mandla smiled. 'No,' he said, 'I feel safer on the land, but thank you.'

Once again Tokoloshe felt the strange pain that had disturbed him before and he saw the tears roll down Mandla's cheeks. But he felt comforted somehow for he knew they were not crocodile tears and, as he turned away, he felt a tear run down his own cheek.

BLAME THE TOKOLOSHE: JACOB'S DREAM

Jacob squatted on the smooth, polished floor of the shed. The dung and mud which he had mixed to plaster the floor had been worn smooth into a patina of cracks and mottled clay. A soft, grey drizzle dripped through the wattle strips he had lashed together to form a roof for the shed.

In a corner, on a heap of straw, lay an emaciated cow; her bulging stomach seemed grotesquely inappropriate on her bony form.

Jacob held a small bowl to her mouth. It contained an evil-smelling mixture, a strong *muthi* provided by the *sangoma,* to drive away the *ubuthakathi.* The cow rolled its eyes and turned its head away from the bowl, breathing heavily.

Jacob sighed wearily. For three days he had hardly moved from her side. His wife had brought him his meals, *phuthu* and meat in a bowl, but she left it near the door, afraid to venture too near the ailing beast in case it passed on the evil spirit to her.

As he squatted beside the cow, the soaking drizzle seemed to seep into his soul and he shivered despite the warm blanket draped over his shoulders. He thought back to the day he had brought the cow home as a young heifer, and further back, to the days he didn't like to think about, when he worked deep below the earth, drilling and burrowing for rock that contained the yellow streaks and veins that drove people mad.

He had spent five years working in the gold mines, but it was no life for a man who loved the smell of the gumtrees and the wattles, who loved to feel the rich, black earth sifting through his fingers when he was planting *mielies,* or digging a furrow for the stream to irrigate his beans.

But he had needed the money to build his house, to pay *ilobola* for his wife and to buy a cow and a goat to set himself up as a farmer. So he had made a decision that he would spend five years working in the mines, saving every penny he could, and then return to lead the life he loved with a partner he could grow to love.

There were memories he tried to erase from his mind, but they kept flooding back: the hostels – where the men slept and ate – that smelled of sweat and drink.

Although by nature a quiet and thoughtful man, it was good in a place like that to belong to a group and he was a member of the *Mkhize* tribe, of whom there were a fair number working with him, so he was never lonely.

He had few happy memories of the years spent slaving on the mines. However, one of them was his introduction to gumboot dancing. He had joined a group under the tutelage of one of the champion gumboot dancers on the Reef. Jacob proved to have a strong sense of rhythm and an immediate grasp of the intricacies of the dance-form and he soon became the leader of the group.

His most prized possession was the trophy they had received when they won the championship – a large, inscribed, silver gumboot. It stood near his bed, together with his polished football boots and his scarf with the Manchester United badge.

He had returned to the land of his birth, KwaZulu-Natal, to an area called Umbumbulu, and, on a hill overlooking a lush valley, had built his home – a spacious thatched hut with a small shed for the cow and goat he intended to buy.

It was only when he had created his home and acquired his livestock that he felt secure enough to visit the parents of his wife and present them with the *ilobola* they required.

Everything seemed to be happening as he had planned; his wife was happy and was proud of her husband and their home. They both wished for a little boy who would grow up to help his father till the land and grow the crops.

But Jacob soon discovered fate had a way of confounding his deepest desires. After two years they still had no children and his wife gradually acquired a sullen and morose disposition. Joseph was concerned, but nothing he did or said seemed to lighten her heart or her spirit and she became a bitter woman.

She visited the *sangoma* who lived in a large house near the village. She was convinced she couldn't have children because of the Tokoloshe and she wanted some *muthi* to drive him away. On her wrist she wore the band the *sangoma* had given her, made up of bits of fur and skin, and she kept his small bottle of brown liquid close at hand to ward off the evil Tokoloshe.

She combined this belief with a zealous participation in the meetings of a sect called the Zionists. Attired in her green dress with a large white cross, she spent the day singing and praying and would then arrive back home late at night, mumbling and distracted, and collapse on their bed without a word and fall into a deep, troubled sleep.

Now the latest episode in this chapter of disasters embraced his cow. His wife had given him the bottle of *muthi* with a strict injunction to make the cow drink it to drive out the Tokoloshe.

Jacob did not share his wife's beliefs. In truth, he was not a superstitious man; he respected the idea of worshipping the ancestors, but beyond that he held no firm or unshakable belief. He had accepted the bottle and tried to administer the muthi as a measure of his desperation, but now, as he brooded over the heaving form of the sick cow, he felt nothing but despair.

He held his head in his hands and wept. It was something he had never done before – at any rate, not since he was a little boy – but now his whole world had collapsed around him and he was powerless to stop it.

He sobbed great, racking sobs and even his shoulders heaved with his anguish. He threw back his head and cried out: 'You devil Tokoloshe! Why have you done this to me?'

Sitting in the fork of his favourite wild-fig tree, Tokoloshe heard the cry, for you should know by now that Tokoloshes have acute hearing and can hear sounds over vast distances. He shook his head and sighed. 'It is always my fault,' he thought sadly. 'Whenever something terrible happens, I am blamed. Of course, that's how I got my reputation!'

He decided he should investigate this latest outrage attributed to him. So he rubbed his magic pebble and became invisible and as light as air, and in this invisible state, he allowed himself to be borne by the wind and the rain until he reached the shed where Jacob was hunched over the sick cow.

He settled soundlessly near the cow and took in the scene instantly. The cow was very sick and he had been blamed, but there was something else; the man was feeling great pain and distress and it wasn't just because of the cow!

Tokoloshe studied the man closely. The rain had soaked his blanket and was trickling through his hair and beard, but he was in another world, a world with small children who clung to him and laughed. Tokoloshe saw the children of the man's dreams and understood his pain.

He decided to look at the sick cow and see what he could do. He crouched before the cow and looked into her large, brown eyes, for it is another fact of Tokoloshe lore that Tokoloshes can speak to and understand others by looking into their eyes.

The cow said to him plainly and clearly: 'I have great pain; I have not much longer in this world.'

Tokoloshe smiled and shook his head, then he carefully laid his hands on her distended stomach. His bony fingers seemed to pulse with energy and sparks flickered from their tips, seeming to penetrate the cow. Slowly the swollen stomach receded and assumed a normal size.

The cow lifted her head and gazed gratefully at Tokoloshe. Her eyes said: 'You have stopped the pain, I am well again'. And she struggled to turn onto her side. Tokoloshe grinned and his eyes sparkled as only a Tokoloshe's eyes can sparkle.

Jacob looked up as the cow moved and then slowly stood, astonished at what he saw. The cow was tossing her head and then slowly she rose to her feet and stood unsteadily before him. She was no longer sick and she rubbed her nose against his arm to tell him so.

Jacob could not believe his eyes; he laughed and cried with joy at the same time. He turned towards the door to call his wife and, at that moment, Tokoloshe decided to show himself.

Jacob stepped back in alarm as the form of the Tokoloshe materialized before him, but Tokoloshe held up his hand and then, grinning his mischievous grin, he pointed at the cow. The cow gave a long 'moo' and tossed her head. Then Tokoloshe rubbed his magic pebble and was gone.

Jacob glanced down at the bowl of *muthi* he had put out for the cow and he strode to it and kicked it across the shed, spilling the contents on the floor. He decided from that moment he would try to find a way to teach his wife the truth about the Tokoloshe, even if it took him the rest of his life.

Back in the fork of his tree, Tokoloshe enjoyed a warm feeling of satisfaction, for he had cleared his name of one injustice, even though there were hundreds of others.

ILOBOLA

Everything about Joseph Shabalala was 'cool' – well, almost everything; his Ray-Ban 'shades' were cool, his cream-coloured, designer panama hat was cool, his imitation brushed-suede jacket was cool and, of course, his two-tone shoes with leather uppers were cool.

When he drove about in his secondhand Ford Thunderbird with personalized number plates, he was a real 'cool dude', and he had sparkling, white teeth and a ready smile to go with his cool demeanour.

There was only one small blemish, one tiny flaw that stood in the way of his being cool in every way; his eyes were small and mean and when he flashed his ready smile those eyes remained small and mean.

He was like a beautiful package but, when you unwrapped it, there was something ugly inside, because Joseph was a rent-collector. In his head there was a calculator that was incessantly adding up and subtracting, making sums and adding interest.

The personalized number plates on his car read 'LUCKY 1', because Joseph was nicknamed 'Lucky' and he accepted this label without complaint; in fact, he signed himself as 'Lucky Joseph Shabalala' in all his correspondence.

He was smiling now as he drove deftly with one hand on the steering wheel, swerving for the potholes that appeared with regularity on the narrow, tarred road that wound through KwaMashu.

The township had spawned many shacks years ago, when people were forced to live in separate areas, and now that there was no longer any restriction, most people still stayed there because they couldn't afford to move elsewhere.

Some unscrupulous entrepreneurs, such as Lucky Joseph Shabalala, had bought up some of the houses as people moved out and were charging exorbitant rents for them. Lucky had just visited three of his tenants to collect his rent and was on his way to the fourth and last one of the day.

On the seat next to him lay his black leather briefcase – no one would have guessed that it was imitation leather – stuffed with bank notes from the rent he had just collected; his spirits were soaring and he had good cause to be smiling as he drove with elan along the winding road.

His final visit was to a house situated on the outskirts of KwaMashu, where the tenant was a Mr. Solomon Nokwe. Lucky Shabalala smiled more broadly and his teeth sparkled more brightly as he thought of Solomon Nokwe's problems. The poor man had been

retrenched and had been out of work for some months ; the result was that he owed Lucky Shabalala three months' rent and faced the very real possibility of eviction.

But this was not the reason Lucky Shabalala smiled so broadly; after all, he was not an unfeeling man. No, he smiled broadly because he thought of Solomon Nokwe's pretty daughter, Thandi, who had taken his fancy some months ago. She had resisted all his overtures and he couldn't understand why, because he had everything to offer – looks, style and wealth.

Then he discovered she had a childhood sweetheart, a young man named Welcome, who lived nearby with his parents. After further enquiries he discovered the family was poor and the boy was out of work. And now he had devised a clever strategy that would make it impossible for Thandi to reject his advances.

He turned up the car radio to full volume and happily drove in a blast of music, along the narrow road to his final destination for the day.

Solomon Nokwe had tried to find work for months. He had worked as a fork-lift operator for a large storage company but, as his employers had explained to him, times were hard, losses were heavy and they had had no alternative but to retrench a large portion of their workforce and so, after twenty years of loyal service, Solomon had found himself without a job.

He had spent months visiting employment agencies, standing in queues and even going from door to door, but nobody seemed interested in a fifty-year-old fork-lift operator. His retrenchment package was swiftly running out and because of his situation, he had fallen behind in his rent and even despaired of having enough money to buy food for his family in the coming months. His wife was a loyal, loving woman who had taken on a part-time job as a domestic help and without her contribution they would never have survived.

Thandi, too, did everything she could to help, but she was in her final year at the local high school and was studying hard to pass her examinations. Nonetheless, over weekends she worked at the local supermarket to help her father.

Her close friend, Welcome, had been her constant companion since they were small children and it seemed only natural as they grew up that they would come to be even closer friends. They shared all their secrets, their joys and their fears. Thandi was distressed beyond measure by her father's retrenchment; she knew he was a proud man and she saw him slowly become more and more depressed by his circumstances.

She had also told Welcome of her father's problems with the rent and of the visits of the flashy rent-collector. When she told him about how Lucky Shabalala had tried to take advantage of her, young Welcome became very angry and vowed to teach him a lesson. It was only after she had explained her father's predicament that he promised not to do anything foolish that would make matters worse.

He did, however, speak to his friend, Jabulani, who had told him of some very strange happenings that involved a Tokoloshe, whom he had caught in the shape of a fish and who had subsequently helped him with his problems.

Jabulani listened attentively to Welcome's account of Mr. Nokwe's problems and of his daughter Thandi's difficulties with Lucky Shabalala, who owned the house and who was owed three months' rent.

'Do you think your Tokoloshe would help us?' Welcome asked anxiously.

'I don't know; I don't even know how to summon him,' said Jabulani. 'He just appeared in the shape of a fish. He helped me because I set him free.'

'I have heard,' said Welcome, 'that Tokoloshes will hear you if you call them at the stream where they live and if there is a chance of some mischief they're unable to resist it.'

'I'll show you where I caught the fish,' said Jabulani, 'and you can try calling him.'

That afternoon, after school, Jabulani took Welcome to the deep pool near the footbridge and as they stood in the shade of the willows Jabulani took his leave. 'I think it would be better if you called him alone,' he said. 'Tokoloshes are very nervous and he might not come with two of us here.'

After he'd left, Welcome stood uncertainly on the grassy bank of the stream; he had never called a Tokoloshe before; in fact he had never even believed in them until Jabulani told him of his experiences. However, he knew that Jabulani would never lie to him.

He felt a little foolish as he knelt down and called across the water: 'Tokoloshe!' He paused. 'Tokoloshe, if you can hear me, please appear, I need your help.'

He scanned the stream anxiously, looking for a fish or some sign the Tokoloshe had heard him, but there was nothing, just the gurgling of the water over the rocks below the bridge and the birds chirping in the trees.

He tried again. 'Tokoloshe, I know of someone who deserves to have some really nasty tricks played on him.' He paused and then continued, 'You can have some good fun and be as mischievous as you like.'

He waited for several minutes, but there was no response. He stood slowly, sighing heavily with disappointment and turned to go, then nearly fell backwards into the stream with astonishment, for squatting on the grass before him was the weirdest little creature, half monkey and half human; its bright, glittering eyes regarded him with suspicion. Welcome knew immediately this was the Tokoloshe.

'Where did you come from?' he gasped.

'Mischief?' queried the little creature. 'Why do you call on me?'

Welcome wanted to pinch himself to make sure he was not dreaming, but instead he said: 'My friend Jabulani told me how you helped him after he had set you free...' He paused because there was no response from the little creature, then he added, 'You were a fish and he caught you and then set you free.'

Suddenly Tokoloshe's face lit up into a broad grin and he said, 'Football!' and at that a football appeared at his feet and, aiming a sharp kick at the ball, he sent it whizzing like a bullet at Welcome. The ball struck Welcome in the stomach and hurtled him backwards into the stream. He landed with a yell and a splash and Tokoloshe rolled about on the grass, chattering with laughter.

Welcome stood up in the stream, which was quite shallow, controlling his anger. 'I need your help,' he said, 'and you can have some fun at the same time.'

Tokoloshe's smile became even broader. 'Don't you like the water?' he asked mischievously. 'Come into the sun and you'll dry out,' and he chattered with laughter yet again.

Welcome climbed out of the stream, his clothes dripping and uncomfortable. 'Will you help me?' he asked.

Tokoloshe squatted on his haunches again. 'I had fun with your friend,' he said, 'and, of course, he set me free, so maybe I'll help you for his sake.'

'Thank you,' said Welcome and he told the Tokoloshe all about Mr. Nokwe's troubles and about the flashy rent-collector, Lucky Shabalala, who was set to evict his tenant because he owed three months' rent.

'What else?' asked Tokoloshe mischievously, because being a Tokoloshe, he knew at once that Welcome hadn't told him everything.

Welcome lowered his head in embarrassment. 'He has also made advances on Mr. Nokwe's daughter, Thandi...' he paused and Tokoloshe regarded him quizzically, '...and Thandi and I have been friends for many years...,' still Tokoloshe waited, '...and we plan to get married as soon as I can get a job,' concluded Welcome lamely.

Tokoloshe grinned: 'And you think he will use the hold he has over Mr. Nokwe to get to her?'

Welcome nodded glumly; he was disconcerted by the Tokoloshe's astute grasp of the situation.

Tokoloshe jumped up. 'Well, it does sound like fun,' he chortled. 'I think we should teach this Lucky Shabalala a lesson he won't forget.'

'I'll show you where Mr. Nokwe lives,' said Welcome with a sense of relief.

'No need,' said Tokoloshe, 'I know everything,' and he bounded into the stream and disappeared with a splash and a flicker of light.

Welcome rubbed his eyes and wondered whether he had dreamed it all, then he remembered Jabulani had said the same thing. 'It was like a dream,' he had said.

He set off for home with a spring in his step and with hope in his heart.

Lucky drew up in front of Solomon Nokwe's house. It was a drab, rectangular structure with a grey, corrugated, asbestos roof. As with all the other houses in KwaMashu it had been built with economy and utility in mind. The houses had one or two bedrooms, with essential facilities such as a small kitchen, a small living-room and a very small bathroom and toilet combined.

Lucky noticed a movement at the curtains as he got out of the car and knew he had been seen. He took his time locking the car and adjusting his hat and shades in the side mirror of the car. It was good psychology to keep them waiting, he thought.

Before the front door a small, hairy creature squatted, watching him with a merciless glint in its eye. It was the Tokoloshe – only he was invisible.

Lucky walked slowly towards the front door with briefcase in hand, over the concrete slab spanning the ditch that served as a gutter. As he stepped onto the slab the soles of his two-tone shoes with leather uppers suddenly seemed to become as smooth and slippery as soap and his feet shot out from under him, sending him sprawling into the ditch.

Tokoloshe rolled over with silent laughter, hardly able to contain himself. Lucky scrambled up out of the ditch as the front door opened and Mrs. Nokwe rushed out to help him. '*Awu*, Mr. Shabalala,' she said, 'what a terrible thing! Did you hurt yourself?'

'Don't worry, it was just a small accident,' he muttered, attempting to wipe off a huge mud stain that covered his jacket and his trousers. His cream-coloured, designer panama hat lay in the ditch where he had fallen.

'I'll get it,' said Mrs. Nokwe, moving towards the ditch, but Lucky stopped her. 'Don't worry,' he said, trying to regain his composure, 'I can manage.' But, as he bent down to reach for his hat in the ditch, another strange thing happened: he seemed to lose his footing again and plunged head first into the ditch once more.

Tokoloshe squatted beside the ditch, watching the result of his well-timed push, with great delight.

Solomon Nokwe and Thandi emerged from the house at the sound of the commotion to witness the sight of Lucky Shabalala, covered in mud from head to foot, crawling out of the ditch; there was mud in his eyes and in his mouth and he spluttered and staggered as he tried to clean it off.

'Come inside, and you can clean yourself up,' said Mrs. Nokwe, alarmed in case he had been drinking.

'What happened?' asked Solomon Nokwe in amazement.

'I'm going to write a letter to the authorities,' fumed Lucky. 'These gutters are a disgrace,' he continued, removing a lump of mud from his head. 'They're a danger to the public.'

Mrs. Nokwe picked up the briefcase, which lay beside the ditch, but Lucky snatched it from her and they went inside with Lucky leaving a trail of mud behind him.

Tokoloshe slipped in after them, just before Mrs. Nokwe closed the door. 'Give me your jacket, Mr. Shabalala,' she said, 'and I'll try to clean it.'

'Thank you,' said Lucky, putting down his briefcase and handing her the jacket. He turned to Solomon Nokwe. 'Mr. Nokwe, could I speak to you in private?' he said and, bowing deeply with what he hoped was a winning smile, added, 'That is, if the ladies don't mind.' Thandi turned abruptly on her heel and left the room with Mrs. Nokwe following.

Tokoloshe was now sitting on top of the crockery cupboard with his feet dangling over the edge.

Solomon Nokwe cleared his throat. 'Mr. Shabalala,' he began, intending to explain his difficulties in paying the rent, but Lucky held up a hand. 'Please,' he interrupted, 'I don't want to talk about the rent, not just yet.'

He paused and smiled, only in his muddy condition the smile wasn't very cool and, as has been mentioned, his eyes remained small and mean.

'I have a business proposition for you,' he said suavely. 'What would you say if I tore up the rental agreement and allowed you to stay in this charming, little house free of charge?'

'Free of charge?' repeated Solomon Nokwe, bewildered.

'Just think,' continued Lucky, 'no more worries, even when you are out of work, like you are now.'

'I intend to find work,' said Solomon Nokwe firmly.

'Of course you do,' said Lucky sympathetically, 'but as you know, times are hard, aren't they?' He paused again, smiling, then said quite callously, 'I will give you R3 000 for *ilobola*,' and he picked up his briefcase, which was beside him. 'I have the money here.'

'*Ilobola?*' Solomon Nokwe stood up angrily.

'Of course, your daughter would have to agree,' said Lucky hastily, 'I would never dream of forcing my affections on her.' He opened the briefcase. 'It's simply a business proposition; the house is yours, and R3 000.' He paused again, then said mournfully: 'Think of the alternative: your poor wife and daughter, no home, no work and no money.'

Solomon Nokwe's face was grim and he said tightly: 'My daughter already has a boyfriend.'

'And they intend to get married as soon as he finds work,' added Lucky sarcastically, 'of course.' He paused and laid a hand on Solomon Nokwe's shoulder. 'Why don't you give her a little advice?' he whispered. 'Will he ever be able to give you *ilobola* like this?' and he turned the briefcase upside down and emptied the contents on the table.

Tokoloshe jumped soundlessly down from the wardrobe and squatted on the corner of the table.

Solomon Nokwe moved to the table and gazed at the contents of the briefcase. 'Is this some kind of joke?' he asked.

Lucky, whose eyes had been fixed triumphantly on Solomon Nokwe, looked down at the table and then stood frozen in disbelief. Lying on the table was a large pile of blank sheets of paper, the size of banknotes.

He rushed to the table and grabbed a handful. 'I don't understand,' he said in a strangled voice. 'I had all my rent money in here.'

Tokoloshe pointed a bony finger at the papers in Lucky's hand; Lucky gasped aloud and threw them down as if they were on fire. On the blank notes, as if drawn by a child, appeared a face with a wide grin from ear to ear and large round eyes, with the word 'Tokoloshe' scrawled beneath it.

Lucky backed towards the door. 'It's the Tokoloshe,' he muttered. 'This house is bewitched.' Then he turned and ran towards his car.

Solomon Nokwe followed him out. 'Wait,' he said, 'what about your briefcase, your hat, your jacket?'

But Lucky was in no mood to listen. He turned the key in the ignition, but instead of the roar of his powerful V8 engine, there was a huge explosion and the bonnet of his car blasted into the air followed by clouds of black smoke. He scrambled out of the smoking car and, as he did so, the two tyres near him exploded with a bang, sending him backwards into the ditch for the third time.

Tokoloshe was by this time almost paralytic with laughter; he rolled about and kicked his heels in the air with delight.

Lucky scrambled out of the ditch, totally hysterical and incoherent, and as the Nokwe family appeared on the doorstep he turned and ran blindly up the road. That was the last they ever saw of him.

When Welcome came to visit, Thandi started telling him about the amazing happenings, but he stopped her, saying: 'I know, it was the Tokoloshe,' and she looked at him in amazement.

Back at his stream, Tokoloshe chattered again with laughter. 'That was good *ilobola*,' he said, and leaped like a silver trout into the water.

MAD ESTHER

The land was in the grip of a fierce drought; it gripped the streams and rivers and squeezed them dry; it gripped the farmer's fields until their *mielies* and other crops were strangled and shrivelled into dry, brown stumps. It gripped the trees, the grass and every leafy plant and reduced them to lifeless stubble.

With the drought came the heat; every day the sun rose like a red ball of fire and the bellows of the African furnace blew until it became white-hot and spread its radiance over the land.

Two summers and winters had passed without a drop of rain. *Worst drought in living memory,* screamed the headlines, but Tokoloshe could remember times like these, long before most of the big ones were born, when he had gone deep into the earth and found an underground pool or river, where he sheltered until the rains came again.

He remembered a time when the land was so dry fires raged through the forests and all the animals fled in panic from the roaring flames, too terrified to care about who their fellow fugitives were; buck and deer fled side by side with lions and other predators, and Tokoloshe fled with them.

When he returned to his stream after the rains came he didn't recognize his surroundings, for the trees had been reduced to black, burnt-out skeletons. But he knew that after two summers the green leaves would return, new shoots would appear and life would start again. Tokoloshe knew that life continued, no matter what catastrophes occurred.

His deep pool beneath the willows had now shrunk to the size of a pond, and he could no longer splash and frolic in the sparkling stream for it was just a trickle.

He spent much of his time rescuing fish that had been marooned in the mud and taking them to deeper water, but many of them perished on the muddy banks of the stream, where only the barbel, or catfish, could survive, for they could remain embedded in the mud for months without any problem.

But there were others who suffered from the drought; the big ones could no longer fill their buckets from the stream. In their homes and at their work there was no water as the tanks had run dry and they had to queue for hours twice a week, waiting with their buckets for the corporation tanker that came to dispense emergency water.

Esther was an old woman who lived on her own in a shack made of corrugated iron and cardboard. Everybody called her 'Mad Esther' for she went about muttering to herself and sometimes cackled with laughter for no apparent reason. But the main reason for referring to her as 'Mad Esther' was that her conversation had stuck at the number 'ninety-nine'.

If anyone asked her anything or greeted her she would respond with 'ninety-nine'. And if she became angry or needed to talk about anything, she would say 'ninety-nine' five or six times. To herself she was saying, 'The drought is bad, everything is dying.' However, to others she was saying 'Ninety-nine, ninety-nine, ninety-nine.'

Tokoloshe was the only one who understood her. As with the children of the village, she accepted him without question and would greet him with 'ninety-nine' and he would respond: 'Yes, it's very hot, *Gogo*,' for he heard what was in her mind, not what was on her tongue.

He made sure she always had some water and something to eat in her shack and she accepted his river-food without question.

Esther had a cat called Madumbie who followed her about like a dog. Esther named her Madumbie because she was pear-shaped and spiky and her fur stuck out in tufts just like the spikes on the *madumbie*. When Esther cooked her favourite meal – *madumbies* with *maas* – she would point at her cat and call out, 'Ninety-nine,' meaning 'I'm eating *madumbies*,' and then cackle with laughter.

When she shuffled to the village store every Monday morning to buy her milk for the week, Madumbie would walk behind her. When she went into the store and put her coins on the counter for the milk, Madumbie would sit outside the door waiting for her and then the two of them would return to the shack, one behind the other.

On the Monday our story begins, it seemed as if it had been hot and windless forever and the sun baked the earth into a dry crust.

MAD ESTHER

Esther had set out early to avoid the heat of the day, for she preferred to sit on the shady verandah of the store waiting for it to open rather than endure the merciless sun. She shuffled along under a tattered, black umbrella which, like the handbag she clutched, was a discarded relic she had found on a rubbish dump.

Madumbie padded behind her and the two of them trailed along, for all the world like a witch with her cat.

On the same day, Tokoloshe decided to pay her a visit to check that all was well, but when he reached the shack he found it empty and he remembered that Monday was her milk day. He rolled over in irritation with himself for being so forgetful, then, shaking the dust from his fur, he set off towards the store.

As he neared the village he saw Esther lying, moaning, in the path before him. Madumbie was high up in the branches of a nearby tree and when she saw Tokoloshe she slithered down and ran up to him yowling, for Madumbie didn't miaow like other cats, she caterwauled.

'All right, Madumbie,' said Tokoloshe as he knelt beside Esther, 'let her tell me what happened.'

Esther had a bruise on her cheek, but otherwise was unharmed. 'Ninety-nine, ninety-nine, ninety-nine,' she moaned as Tokoloshe helped her up.

'Two big ones attacked you and took your handbag,' he repeated. 'How long ago?'

'Ninety-nine,' replied Esther.

'Just before I arrived,' repeated Tokoloshe and he patted her hand. 'You go home with Madumbie,' he said, grim-faced, 'I'll deal with this.'

'Ninety-nine,' said Esther as she moved off with Madumbie.

'Yes, I'll fetch your milk, too,' he said as he watched her shuffle back along the path with Madumbie following.

Tokoloshe was angry and it didn't do for a Tokoloshe to become angry, for his tail started glowing and he started hopping about and tearing the air. He quickly got himself under control, for he knew that whatever he did had to be done dispassionately. He was a Tokoloshe and a Tokoloshe shouldn't feel emotions like anger or sorrow. Laughter, of course, was another thing altogether.

He rubbed his magic pebble and in his invisible state he sped off with his antennae on full alert. He started getting strong vibrations as he approached an old shed with a rusty door hanging on one hinge. He peered in.

Two youths, not quite big ones yet, were crouching in a corner. He recognized them as two local boys who frequently played 'hookey' and spent the day fishing in the stream instead of going to school.

The fat one, who was called Jo-Jo, was holding the bag. 'You didn't have to push her so hard,' he said. 'She's just an old woman.'

'She's not *Gogo*, she's ga-ga,' laughed the other boy, whose name was Stompie because he was short and stocky. 'She's crazy man! C'mon, let's see what's in the bag.'

Jo-Jo turned the bag upside down and a few coins fell to the floor. Stompie grabbed the bag from him and shook it violently. 'There must be more,' he shouted, throwing the bag down. 'We've watched her every week and every week she has money for milk.'

'Well, it must be in her shack,' said Jo-Jo, 'maybe she has it buried there.'

At that moment the bag started moving and the two boys leaped up.

'There's something in the bag,' whispered Jo-Jo.

'There's nothing in the bag,' replied Stompie vehemently. 'I've just shaken it out.'

'Well, it moved,' whispered Jo-Jo, backing towards the door.

'Rubbish, it was just the leather stretching or something,' said Stompie and he picked up the bag. As he did so, a long, black snake with beady eyes uncoiled itself and slithered out. Stompie dropped the bag like a hot potato and the two boys ran towards the door yelling with terror. But the door was jammed and would not open.

'Open the door!' yelled Jo-Jo, who was fatter and slower than Stompie and therefore lagged behind him.

'I can't,' yelled Stompie frantically, 'it's jammed.'

The two boys turned and froze in terror as the vicious-looking reptile snaked towards them, hissing and rearing its head. Jo-Jo flung Stompie aside and tried to force the door open with all his might. But it wouldn't budge.

They both turned to face the serpent again, their faces pale with terror, when suddenly it hissed: 'I am the Tokoloshe and I can make this serpent strike you now,' and the snake coiled back ready to strike, its eyes glittering venomously.

The two boys screamed and cowered against the door. 'Don't let it strike us,' they begged. 'Please help us.'

'You hurt a harmless, old woman,' hissed the serpent. 'You stole her bag for a few coins,' and its tail flicked the coins across the floor.

'She's mad,' gasped Stompie, 'all she says is "ninety-nine" all day long.'

At this Tokoloshe became so angry he leaped out of the serpent, which slithered away and disappeared into a crack. He rubbed his magic pebble and faced the two boys as he materialized, with his tail glowing and pulsing with anger.

The two boys were even more terrified of Tokoloshe than they were of the serpent, for they knew his power and feared for their lives.

'Mad?' he exclaimed angrily. 'Mad? Did you ever look into her eyes when she said "ninety-nine"? If you had you would have understood perfectly what she was saying, but you are so selfish and greedy you don't care about the spirit that looks through the eyes.'

Jo-Jo stepped forward. 'I am ashamed,' he whispered. 'What can I do now to make amends?'

Tokoloshe turned to Stompie, who had not said a word. 'And you?' he asked.

Stompie nodded. 'Me too,' he said, and then mumbled, 'but I still think she's a bit mad.'

'You will understand one day,' said Tokoloshe and then turned to Jo-Jo. 'What can you do? You can buy her some milk with those coins and you can take the milk to her and tell her you are sorry for what happened.' He turned to Stompie: 'And when she says "ninety-nine" you can look into her eyes and you will understand what she is saying.'

He pointed his finger at them both. 'If you ever again try to harm her, or anyone else, Tokoloshe will know and he will come to you in the shape of a poisonous serpent and this time there will be no escape.'

The door, which had been jammed, suddenly swung loosely on its hinge again and the boys stumbled from the shed protesting they had learned their lesson. Tokoloshe grinned, for he knew it was a lesson they wouldn't forget.

The next day Tokoloshe was lying in his pool, which had shrunk to a muddy pond, trying to keep cool. Being a Tokoloshe he was very sensitive to changes in the atmosphere and all night long he had been aware of unusual waves of energy that swept over him, but he had become so numbed by the stifling heat he didn't dare hope that it signified any change.

Now, suddenly, he became aware of flickering energy high in the heavens and he knew something tremendous was going to happen.

As if to confirm his intuition, the sky began to darken and flickerings of lightning played around the gathering clouds. The rumble of thunder became continuous and the clouds became darker and more ominous; then flashes of lightning lit up the sky and claps of thunder shook the earth.

Tokoloshe leaped up and started dancing around his pool. It was going to rain; the drought was at an end! He chattered with laughter and rolled and splashed in the water.

When the rain started it was a deluge. Leaves and branches were swept down the roads and paths; the streams, which had been barely a trickle, became raging torrents of water and the footbridge over the stream near the willows was swept away. Tokoloshe's pool by the willows was transformed into a huge whirlpool as the water converged on it from all directions.

And in the midst of this deluge Tokoloshe pranced and sang, he chattered and performed cartwheels, he whirled around the whirlpool and he dived and danced on the water; in fact, he had the time of his life for three rain-soaked days.

On the fourth day the rain abated and the sky showed patches of blue, and the sun and the showers of rain mingled. Tokoloshe grinned from ear to ear for when that happened the big ones called it a 'monkey's wedding'.

Tokoloshe ventured out into the world and saw that it was all freshly washed and cleaned. His spirits were high and he decided to pay a visit to Esther. Her shack was on the hill above the village and he knew she would have been quite safe during the storm.

As he approached the shack he saw Esther shuffling quickly towards him. 'Ninety-nine,' she called out anxiously, 'ninety-nine.'

Tokoloshe took her hand. 'What do you say, *Gogo*. Madumbie is missing?'

'Ninety-nine,' she said again.

'I will find her,' said Tokoloshe. 'Go back home, I will bring her to you.'

He turned and streaked off along the path. He knew storms did strange things to some animals; sometimes they would become terrified and run away or hide.

He reached a fork in the path where one branch led to the village, while the other wound down towards the stream. He turned down towards the stream and suddenly his antennae started vibrating strongly. Then he heard a loud caterwauling in the distance and knew he had found Madumbie. She was sitting on a log that had been washed out into the middle of a large pond.

Tokoloshe put his hands on his hips and chattered with laughter. 'How did you get there?' he asked.

Madumbie gave a long yowl, which Tokoloshe understood to mean, 'I was on the log, just about to scoop up a large fish with my paw, when the log started moving.' She gave another yowl: 'And here I am.'

Tokoloshe chattered with laughter again. 'I have a good mind to leave you there,' he said and then, as she gave another yowl, he added, 'all right, don't get your whiskers in a knot,' and pointing a knobbly finger at the log he drew it to the bank with ease.

Madumbie leaped off and raced along the path towards the little shack. Tokoloshe followed and as he approached the shack he saw Esther standing in the path with Madumbie in her arms, but even more wonderful was the brilliant rainbow that arched over the shack.

'Ooooooh,' gasped Tokoloshe in wonder and he raced to the foot of the rainbow and rubbed his magic pebble. Esther cackled with laughter as Tokoloshe dissolved and started climbing the rainbow for, in his invisible state, he was composed of energy.

When he reached the top he turned, sat down and tobogganed all the way down, screaming with delight.

As he reached the foot of the rainbow, Esther clapped her hands and cackled with laughter. 'Ninety-nine!' she shrieked.

'I hope you never reach a hundred,' said Tokoloshe, smiling happily.

THE HELPING HAND

There were three models for sale: the De Luxe model (ESP 100), the All Purpose model (FV 50), and the Utility model (GV 25). You would be forgiven for thinking that these were motorcars or motorcycles that were for sale, but you would be astonished to discover, on reading the large black and gold letters emblazoned on the plate-glass windows in which the models were displayed, that they were, in fact, coffins, for the lettering read: 'The Helping Hand Funeral Parlour'.

PART ONE: THE HELPING HAND FUNERAL PARLOUR

Doctor Malinga glowed with pride each morning when he unlocked the heavy, wooden doors and walked into the tastefully furnished waiting room with a large vase of white, artificial roses on the receptionist's desk.

His mother had been so impressed with Dr. Rosenberg's new surgery that opened in the village just before her child was born that she named her child Doctor, in the belief that the name would bring him similar good fortune.

As he grew up, people were naturally impressed when he signed himself 'Doctor Malinga' and he did nothing to dispel their misconception. Doctor Malinga discovered it was much more lucrative to devote himself to the dead than to the living, so he opened The Helping Hand Funeral Parlour. And it flourished.

He catered for all tastes and all pockets; the De Luxe model (ESP 100), meaning Extra Special 100%, was a splendid coffin made of Kiaat, a beautifully grained, local hardwood, with solid brass fittings and a hinged section at the head for viewing. It was lined in purple velvet and was his pride and joy.

He thought of putting a sign next to it which read, 'Say Farewell in Style', but thought better of it, deciding to let the coffin speak for itself. The price was variable, depending on the status and affluence of his customers, but it was always expensive.

The All Purpose model (FV 50), meaning Fantastic Value 50%, was also impressive, but the timber was veneered and the fittings were brass-plated, and, of course, the lining was satin, not velvet, and there was no viewing section. Still, it was a popular seller.

His biggest money-spinner, however, was the Utility model (GV 25), meaning Good Value 25%. Made of knotted pine, it had plastic fittings and no lining whatsoever. Doctor Malinga had borrowed a maxim from a local car-hire firm, for on a card next to the coffin was a sign that read: 'No fuss, no frills, just plain, good value'.

On the morning our story starts, the fog was so heavy Doctor Malinga couldn't even read the sign on his window as he approached the showroom; in fact, he couldn't see more than a metre ahead of him.

It's a 'pea-soup' fog thought Doctor Malinga as he unlocked the door and heard the tinkling chime he had installed to alert him when customers entered. It played the first strain of a popular lullaby, 'Tula, tu'lala baba, lala sana', meaning 'Be still my child, sleep sweetly', which he thought was most appropriate.

He arrived early this particular morning because his receptionist had telephoned to say she was not feeling well and would stay in bed for the day. He was irritated because he was expecting a consignment of coffins from a factory near the Transkei border and would now have to deal with it personally.

He was running very low on stock and he couldn't afford to be caught empty-handed; besides, he felt that it showed disrespect for the departed. He sat back in his swivel chair at his dark mahogany desk, with the morning paper and a cup of coffee, to await the delivery of his precious consignment.

PART TWO: A PERFECT SOLUTION

Perfect Malimela peered through the windscreen of his bakkie, attempting to penetrate the thick fog that blanketed and obscured everything before him. He had 'crawled' for the last ten kilometres and on a number of occasions had had to brake suddenly as a tree or a bush loomed before him. He couldn't see the road more than a metre ahead, even with his bright lights on.

He thought of pulling to the side of the road to wait for the fog to lift, but he knew fogs like these sometimes lasted for days and he couldn't afford to be stranded, even for half a day. He had a precious consignment of coffins in the back of his bakkie he had promised to deliver that very day and he was still a good way from his destination.

Like Doctor Malinga's mother, Perfect's mother had named him on a sudden impulse; she stared at her new-born baby in wonder and whispered: 'He's perfect,' and he was, forever after, Perfect Malimela, though he found it a continuous struggle to live up to his name.

At that moment he felt far from perfect and was, in fact, in a foul mood. His misfortunes had multiplied ever since he set off from the factory the previous day with his load and then discovered after a few kilometres that he had a flat tyre. This was not the worst of his ills, for he then discovered his spare tyre was also flat and he had to walk to the service station, a few kilometres further on, to have it repaired.

After a restless night sleeping in his bakkie at the side of the road, he awoke to find the world shrouded in a blanket of fog so heavy he couldn't see his hand in front of his face.

He revved the bakkie a few times to vent his ire and then drove slowly on along the dirt road towards The Helping Hand Funeral Parlour.

As he rounded a bend, he realised too late that it was sharper than he thought and the bakkie veered off the road into a deep ditch, pitching over onto its side and spilling the coffins onto a grassy bank which dropped away steeply to the stream below. The coffins slid down the slope, gathering momentum as they went, like some macabre go-kart race in the underworld, until they torpedoed into the stream with a mighty splash.

Two were splintered on impact, but most bobbed merrily on down the stream, like a fleet of strange vessels. All this happened in an instant and it was all because of the thick fog.

Perfect clambered out of the bakkie cursing; he wasn't hurt and the bakkie didn't appear to be damaged, but he'd need help to get it on the road again. Because of the poor visibility, he didn't notice the coffins were no longer stacked in the back and, with his mood blacker than ever, he set off on the long trudge back to the filling station for some help.

PART THREE: LITTLE BOXES

Tokoloshe danced in the fog; it was like a soft, comforting blanket that enveloped him when he moved and he made little eddies of fog swirl around him as he danced.

Unlike other creatures, Tokoloshes can see through the thickest fog with their extrasensory perception and Tokoloshe danced to express his joy at seeing the world transformed into a gossamer fairyland.

As he turned and twisted in this white world, his feet barely touched the stream, for he became one with the swirling mist and his spirit soared with the joy of being.

But his rapturous dance was interrupted by a strange sight. Through the swirling fog he saw a fleet of unusual craft bobbing towards him. They were long boxes of varying sizes; some with beautiful golden handles and others without any embellishment, but all of them looked ready to be boarded and to be sailed into the sunset or, in the present circumstances, into the fog. 'Ooooooh!' Tokoloshe gave vent

to his sense of wonder and excitement at seeing such a magical sight, and he boarded the nearest one, which was a splendid vessel with large, golden handles and, standing astride it like the captain of a galleon, he guided it towards the bank under the willows.

The other boxes bobbed on merrily down the stream and disappeared into the fog.

Tokoloshe jumped off his craft and examined it carefully from top to bottom. The timber was dark and beautifully polished and the box itself tapered towards one end, which he decided was the front of the vessel. At the back, which was wider, there were some shiny hinges and a small handle and Tokoloshe decided this must be the door that led down into the vessel.

He decided at once to investigate and opened the door very carefully so as not to disturb the occupants and peered in. Although it was gloomy inside, his sharp eyes immediately saw it was empty and he wondered why the crew had left such a beautiful vessel unattended.

Well, now it was his, he thought with pride, and he would take good care of it. He climbed down into the vessel and ran his fingers over the soft velvet that covered the timber inside and once again he gasped in delight: 'Oooooh!' It felt like the silkiest feathers on a duck's back.

It was so warm and cosy inside that Tokoloshe decided he would lie down and have a nap in his new vessel and soon he was dreaming Tokoloshe dreams of marvellous mischief.

PART FOUR: TOKOLOSHE MISCHIEF

Moses decided to visit some old friends he had not seen for a long time and they sat up late into the night talking about old times and, naturally, they enjoyed a few draughts together from a calabash. He left in the early hours of the morning and had a good three-mile walk along the stream to reach his home.

By this time the fog was already rolling in and Moses found it difficult to get his bearings. After a while he realised he had strayed from the path and was hopelessly lost. He decided to shelter under a thick bush for the night and wait until morning when, with a clear head and with the light of dawn, he would soon be able to find his way home.

He slept fairly comfortably for, after years of herding cattle and sheep, he was used to sleeping out in the open and his thick overcoat kept him warm and comfortable.

But when he awoke the following morning the fog was still so heavy he decided to wait where he was until it cleared.

By mid-morning it started to lift and Moses decided it was time to set off. Although the world was still swathed in mist, it was nothing like the heavy fog that had obscured everything and he was soon able to find the stream and the path that would take him home.

In no time he reached the footbridge that spanned the stream and, as he crossed it, he glanced down at the pool below and then stopped in astonishment. Lying on the muddy bank was a polished coffin with large brass handles. He rubbed his eyes and shook his head to make sure he was not still confused from his night out, but it was still there.

He crossed the bridge and clambered down to the stream, knelt before the coffin, touched the smooth, polished timber and tapped on it with his knuckles.

As he did so, the viewing aperture suddenly snapped open and, peering up at him, was a small head with large eyes, which Moses took to be the shrunken head of a corpse.

He backed away from the horrifying sight and then, as the corpse sat up, screamed in terror and took to his heels, scrambling up the bank and along the path as fast as his legs would carry him. He never stopped running until he reached his home, locking himself in and staying there for a week to recover from his ordeal.

Meanwhile, Tokoloshe discovered the upper deck of his vessel was hinged from top to bottom and, if he gave a mighty shove from within, it would flap open and allow him to enjoy the passing scene as he floated down the stream.

He decided to set off at once, gave his vessel a shove and clambered aboard as it bobbed off under the footbridge and gathered speed as the current swept it along.

The bobbing motion of his vessel and the warm sun made him feel rather sleepy and he pulled the deck cover closed and lay down on the soft, velvet blanket and was soon snorting and grunting, which is what a Tokoloshe does instead of snoring.

PART FIVE: MORE TOKOLOSHE MISCHIEF

By the time Perfect Malimela reached the filling station and managed to persuade the mechanic to drive him to his abandoned bakkie, the fog had already lifted. They reached the bakkie and it was only when Perfect walked around it to inspect the damage that he realised the coffins were missing.

His first thought was that they had been stolen but, when he saw the furrows they had gouged through the muddy terrain as they slid down the slope, he realised what had happened. With an oath he clambered down the slope, calling to the mechanic to wait for him as he followed the tracks, which led him down to the stream and further on to the splintered remains of two of the coffins.

Perfect Malimela was a resourceful man and he quickly calculated that if he could get his bakkie on the road at once and follow the course of the stream as it wound its way along the valley, he might be able to salvage most of the coffins and Doctor Malinga need never know what had happened.

In no time they managed to get the bakkie righted and, after promising the mechanic that he would call in on the way back to settle his bill, he sped off in pursuit of his coffins.

Fortunately, the road ran parallel with the stream for many kilometres and after about an hour he saw the first coffin bobbing along for all the world like a pleasure boat, with its brass handles and hinges shining in the sunlight.

He was somewhat concerned, for there were no others visible ahead of the solitary coffin, but after a further half-hour of frantic driving he saw a whole fleet of them bobbing slowly down the stream. He counted seven and breathed a sigh of relief for, with the solitary coffin some way back and with the two splintered ones, it made a count of ten, which was the number he had set out with.

He would have to think of some excuse for the two missing ones, he thought, but at the moment it didn't concern him; what did concern him was salvaging the wayward coffins.

As already mentioned, Perfect was a resourceful man, and the solution to his problem came to him in a flash. He drove ahead of the floating coffins until he reached a point where the stream narrowed and flowed between two large trees.

He leaped out of the bakkie and strung a tow-rope, which he kept in the bakkie, between the two trees just above the surface of the stream and with the hooked end of the tow-rope held at the ready, he waited for the first coffin to appear.

He did not have long to wait, for it soon came bobbing around the corner of the stream with the others following in a syncopated dance. Their journey was arrested as they encountered the barrier that Perfect had strung across the stream and they bumped into each other, but were held in check by the tow-rope.

Perfect pulled them in, one by one, looping his hook through the handles or over the lid of the coffin, and stacked them carefully in the bakkie. Apart from some mud, which he cleaned off, there was no damage to the polished coffins, but the 'Utility' models, which were not polished, had some dark water stains. Perfect shrugged his shoulders. 'After all', he thought, 'what could you expect if you weren't prepared to pay for quality?'

He sat back in his bakkie and switched on the radio while he waited for the last coffin to appear and, after what seemed an eternity to Perfect, the one remaining coffin came bobbing into sight. 'At last,' thought Perfect as he climbed out of the bakkie and walked towards the barrier he had strung across the stream.

Inside the coffin, Tokoloshe was suddenly awakened with a jolt as his vessel seemed to encounter some obstacle. He pushed up the deck cover and sat up just as Perfect bent down to grasp the handle.

Perfect gasped in horror as the lid of the coffin was suddenly opened from within and then, as a weird creature appeared like a ghoul out of the coffin, he fell backwards into the stream, screaming with terror.

Tokoloshe grinned. That was the second piece of mischief he had wrought from within his vessel, he thought, as he watched the terrified form of Perfect splash out of sight.

PART SIX: THE FINAL RECKONING

Doctor Malinga waited impatiently for his coffins. He made several telephone calls to the factory and each time he was assured the driver and the coffins had left the previous day; the only solution they could offer was that he may have been held up by the fog.

Late that afternoon he received a telephone call from a clearly disturbed driver, who gabbled about spirits and Tokoloshes and told him his coffins were in a bakkie parked near the stream about ten kilometres away and he could fetch them himself.

Doctor Malinga was outraged, but his need for the coffins was greater than his sense of outrage so he sent his handyman, who also drove the hearse on formal occasions, to fetch the coffins and they were brought back, appropriately in a hearse, to The Helping Hand Funeral Parlour, minus the three missing ones.

Meanwhile, Tokoloshe decided it was time to show off his new acquisition and proudly he took old Esther and her cat to see it. When she beheld the coffin with its polished brass handles, she cackled with laughter and said, 'Ninety-nine, ninety-nine, ninety-nine!'

Tokoloshe was incredulous. 'The big ones are put into the box when they stop being and the box is then put deep into the earth? But it's such a lovely box.'

Then he had a thought, for he really felt a strong bond with the old woman who had stopped speaking at number ninety-nine. 'You can have it,' he said, 'when you stop being.'

'Ninety-nine', said Esther angrily, 'ninety-nine!'

'You don't want it?' repeated Tokoloshe. 'But why not?'

'Ninety-nine,' said Esther softly, and her eyes glowed with a strange fire.

'You will dance into the light?' said Tokoloshe wonderingly, then nodded and grinned. 'And Tokoloshe will dance with you,' he said, taking her hand.

And they danced in the twilight; with old Esther shuffling happily and Madumbie yowling as she danced with them.

As they danced, the polished, wooden coffin with its shining brass handles slowly drifted down the stream and was never seen again.

THE HELPING HAND

GLOSSARY

Bakkie:	One-ton, open truck
Boerewors:	Sausage
Braai:	Barbecue
Calabash:	The hollow shell of a gourd, used as a bowl.
Ezeqili:	Trickster tales
Ezezilwane:	Animal tales
Gogo:	Grandmother
Imbuzikazi:	Billy-goat
Inkomazi ezikhala zemithi:	The cow which is the gaps between the branches of the trees, silhouetted against the sky.
Inyanga:	Doctor or herbalist
Isanuzi:	Bee
Izinganekwane:	Folk tales
Jabulani:	Rejoice
KwaMashu:	Township near Durban
Ilobola:	A Zulu tradition where the parents of the bride are given cattle, money or goods for their daughter's hand (dowry).
Maas:	Sour milk

Madumbie (Zulu: idumbe):	Vegetable marrow that grows on a vine
Mandla:	Power
Mantindane:	A small creature, the familiar of a witch
Mielies:	Corn
Mielie-meal porridge:	Porridge made from corn-flour
Mthunzini:	Shady place
Muthi:	Medicine
Ngwenya:	Crocodile
Nyoka:	Snake
Panga:	Broad bush-knife
Phuthu:	Stiff porridge made from cornflour
Samoosa:	Triangular pastry with filling
Samp (Zulu: istambu):	Boiled corn
Sangoma:	Witch-doctor
Shongololos (Zulu: Ameshongololo):	Centipedes
Skelms:	Scoundrels
Stompie:	Shorty
Thandi:	One who is loved
Tokoloshe:	Mischievous imp
Ubuthakathi:	Witchcraft
Voetsek:	Go away (slang)
Waterblommetjiebredie:	Stew made with water-lilies